SHEA SHAKES SHAKESPEARE!

Using th[e] Psychologi[...] magicks in [...] so, and Fae[...]

But tonight Shea, his Faerie-land wife Belphebe, and colleague Vaclav Polacek are *only* attending the theater —until lovelorn Vaclav, smitten with a Shakespearean heroine, zaps all three of them into the world of *The Tempest*. Almost. Because in *this* world, the sorcerer Prospero never arrived—the Isle is in the thrall of foul witch Sycorax, who's turned Ariel into a harpy, and lost sailors into stones. Vaclav turns *himself* into a cow! Unless Harold's magic-math can survive hippos, unicorns, sprites, demons, *things*, fire drakes, lots of goblins, and baby Caliban, Sycorax will turn Shea into shish kebab, and beautiful Belphebe into Bev-B-Que!

And Harold Shea's magic *never* works the way he intends!

CROSSROADS™ ADVENTURES are authorized interactive novels compatible for use with any role-playing game. Constructed by the masters of modern gaming, CROSSROADS™ feature complete rules; *full use* of gaming values—strength, intelligence, wisdom/luck, constitution, dexterity, charisma, and hit points; and multiple pathways for each option; for the most complete experience in gaming books, as fully realized, motivated heroes quest through the most famous worlds of fantasy!

All-new. With an introduction by L. SPRAGUE DE CAMP

ENTER THE ADVENTURE!

TOR'S CROSSROADS™ ADVENTURE SERIES

Dragonharper, based on Anne McCaffrey's Pern
Storm of Dust, based on David Drake's The Dragon Lord
Revolt on Majipoor, based on Robert Silverberg's Majipoor
The Witchfires of Leth, based on C. J. Cherryh's Morgaine
Prospero's Isle, based on L. Sprague de Camp and Fletcher Pratt's The Incomplete Enchanter

COMING SOON

Dzurlord, based on Steve Brust's Jhereg
A Warlock's Blade, based on Christopher Stasheff's Gramarye
Encyclopedia of Xanth, based on Piers Anthony's Xanth
Warhorn, based on Lynn Abbey's Rifkind

A CROSSROADS ADVENTURE

in the World of
L. SPRAGUE DE CAMP and FLETCHER PRATT'S THE INCOMPLETE ENCHANTER

PROSPERO'S ISLE

by Tom Wham

A TOM DOHERTY ASSOCIATES BOOK

This is a work of fiction. All the characters and events portrayed in this book are fictional, and any resemblance to real people or incidents is purely coincidental.

PROSPERO'S ISLE

Copyright © 1987 by Bill Fawcett and Associates

All rights reserved, including the right to reproduce this book or portions thereof in any form.

Crossroads and the Crossroads logo are a trademark of Bill Fawcett and Associates used with permission.

The names, places, and descriptions and other plot elements used in this game are derived from works copyrighted by and trademarked by L. Sprague de Camp. These are used under license and may not be used or reused without L. Sprague de Camp's written permission.

All characters, places, and names in this book are fictitious, and any resemblance to existing persons, places, or things is coincidental.

Crossroads Game/novels are published by Tor Books by arrangement with Bill Fawcett and Associates.

First printing: October 1987

A TOR Book

Published by Tom Doherty Associates, Inc.
49 West 24 Street
New York, N.Y. 10010

Cover art by Doug Beekman
Illustrations by Todd Cameron Hamilton

ISBN: 0-812-56408-1
CAN. ED.: 0-812-56409-X

Printed in the United States of America

0 9 8 7 6 5 4 3 2 1

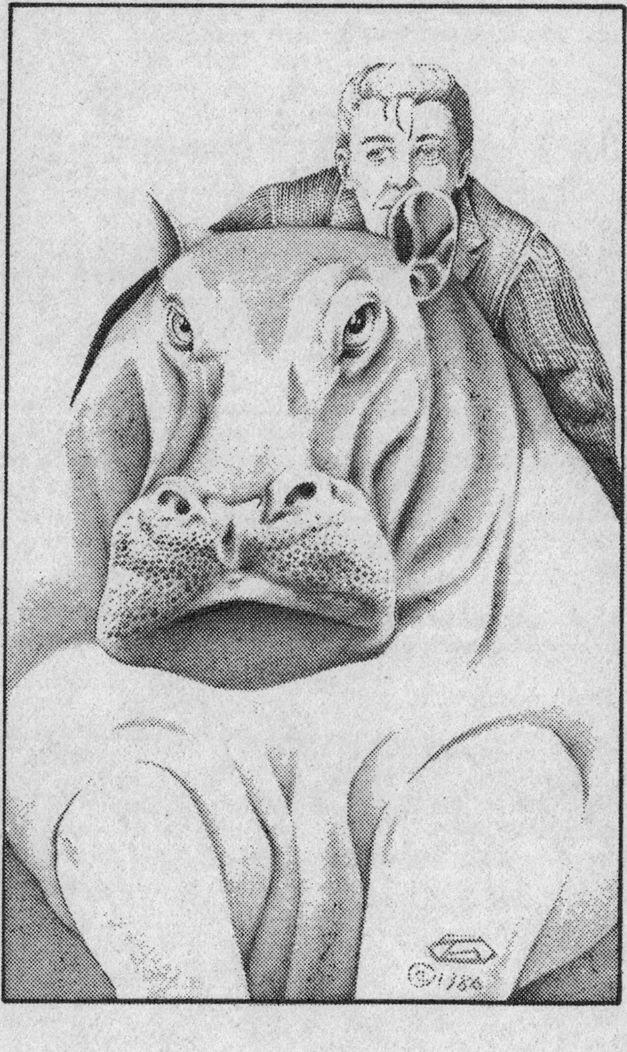

SORCERERS, SYMBOLS, AND SPELLS

MY FRIEND AND collaborator Fletcher Pratt (1897–1957) was a connoisseur and author of heroic fantasy before that term was invented. The son of an upstate New York farmer, Fletcher was born on the Indian reservation near Buffalo—a fact that, he said, entitled him to hunt and fish (though he did neither) in New York State without a license.

As a youth, five feet three but wiry and muscular, Pratt undertook two simultaneous careers in Buffalo. One was as a librarian; the other, that of a prizefighter in the flyweight (112-pound) class. He fought several fights, lost a couple of teeth, and knocked one opponent cold. When the story made the papers, the head librarian told him it would not do to have their employees knocking people about. Forced to choose, Fletcher opted for the library over the ring.

Pratt's college career was cut short by poverty. In the early 1920s, he worked as a reporter on a couple of newspapers. Then he settled in New York with his second wife, the artist Inga Stephens Pratt. (His first wife had tried to compel him to confine his writing to poetry.)

Pratt held several fringe literary jobs, such as editing a "mug book" (a biographical encyclopedia), wherein nonentities paid money to have their pictures and lives included. He also worked for a "writers' institute," which promised to turn every would-be scribbler into a Tolstoy and kept the money rolling in by fulsome flattery of the variest bilge submitted to them. Later, Pratt drew upon these experiences in lecturing about literary rackets.

From 1925 to 1935, Pratt sold science-fiction stories to the science-fiction pulps of the time. He also worked for Hugo Gernsback, then publishing *Wonder Stories*. Pratt translated European science-fiction novels from the French and the German. Gernsback had a way of not paying his authors what he had promised, but Pratt got the better of him. He would translate the first installment or two of a novel and then, when the material was already in print, say: "I'm sorry, Mr. Gernsback, but if you don't pay me, I don't see how I can complete this translation."

He had Gernsback over a barrel. He also took a year off to live in Paris on the insurance money from a fire that gutted the Pratts' apartment. He studied at the Sorbonne, learned languages, and did research for his book on codes and ciphers.

Back in New York, now a self-made scholar of respectable standing, Pratt attacked more serious writing. He hit his stride with histories of the War of 1812 and the American Civil War. The Pratt ménage attracted a wide circle of friends, drawn by Pratt's lavish hospitality and extraordinary sense of fun.

Pratt devised a naval war game, to which his friends were invited monthly. In odd moments he whittled out scale models ($55' = 1''$) of the world's warships, actual and projected, using balsa wood, wires, and pins, until hundreds of models crowded his shelves. In the game, players crawled around the floor, moving their models the distances allowed and writing the estimated ranges of the ships they were shooting at. Then the referees took over the floor, tapemeasuring and calculating damages done to the ships hit. When the Pratts' apartment became too crowded with players, the game was moved to a hall on East 59th Street.

Pratt's interests also included gourmet cookery, on which he wrote a book. He taught at the Bread Loaf Writers' Conference, was a Baker Street Irregular, and served for seven years as president of the New York Authors' Club.

In 1939 my former college roommate, John D. Clark, introduced me to Pratt. I was soon a member of the war-game circle, along with such colleagues as Malcolm Jameson, Ted Sturgeon, and George O. Smith. I had been free-lancing for a year and a half, having lost my job on a trade journal in an economy purge. With the appearance of John W. Campbell's great fantasy magazine *Unknown*, to which I often contributed, Pratt conceived the idea of a series of novels in collaboration with me. I was, naturally, much flattered by this offer from a writer much better-established than I.

The stories would narrate the adventures of a hero who projects himself by symbolic logic into the parallel worlds of myths and legends. I had been studying symbolic logic, and we used my smattering of that science as "corroborative detail, intended to give artistic verisimilitude to an otherwise bald and unconvincing narrative." We made our protagonist a brash, self-assertive young psychologist named Harold Shea. (The name was my choice.)

First, in "The Roaring Trumpet" (*Unknown*, May 1940), we sent Harold to the world of Scandinavian myth. For this story Pratt furnished most of the background, since at that time my knowledge of Norse myth was confined to popular digests and retellings, while Pratt read sagas in the original. I had not yet read the *Heimskringla* and the *Eddas*, with which he was familiar.

For the second episode, in "The Mathematics of Magic" (August 1940), we transferred Harold to the world of Spenser's *Faerie Queene* and let Harold meet his dream girl Belphebe. I was never so enthusiastic about the *Faerie Queene* as Pratt, finding it tedious for long stretches, though long afterward I used a snippet from it in my story "United Imp."

Years later, when I took to light verse, I composed a poem, *The Dragon-Kings*, in Spenserian nine-line stanzas—a very exacting verse form. Having sweated through three such stanzas, I was appalled at the feat of Edmund Spenser, whose *Faerie Queene* comprises over four thousand of the things!

These first two novellas were followed by "The Castle of Iron" (April 1941), which took Harold to the world of Ariosto's *Orlando Furioso* ("mad Roland"). Ludovico Ariosto's tale is livelier than Spenser's; when one of Ariosto's gallant knights rescues a maiden fair from perils dire, he promptly tries to rape her.

In 1941, also, Holt brought out the first two novellas as a cloth-bound book, *The Incomplete Enchanter*, which has been through a number of editions since. We revised and slightly expanded the stories to make more of a unified novel of them. While Pratt proposed the basic themes for the first two stories, those for the later ones were worked out by discussion between us.

The Hitlerian War of 1941–45 caused a hiatus in the Shea saga, while Pratt worked as a war correspondent and I served as an officer in the Naval Reserve. Along with Robert Howard and Isaac Asimov, I performed engineering work for naval aircraft at the Philadelphia Naval Base. (We were not, however, involved in any fictitious "Philadelphia experiment" in making a warship invisible; but I daresay it would have been more fun than running tests on windshield de-icers for airplanes.)

After the war, Pratt and I rewrote and expanded "The Castle of Iron" to book length, in which form it appeared in 1950. We also wrote two more novellas of the saga, placing Harold first in the world of the Finnish *Kalevala* ("The Wall of Serpents") and then in the world of Irish myth ("The Green Magician"). This last *milieu* was the setting whither Harold had intended to go in the first place. After magazine publication (1953–54) these two stories were combined in a book, *Wall of Serpents*, which has been through hard- and soft-backed editions.

In 1976, Ballantine issue a paperback of Harold Shea fantasies, *The Compleat En-*

chanter. The title is a bit of a misnomer, because it includes only the first three of the five Harold Shea stories. The publication of all five in one volume was considered, but the plan was scratched because of the excessive length of such a volume and because of a conflict of contracts. In 1980, Sphere Books put out a British edition of *Wall of Serpents* but changed the title to *The Enchanter Compleated*. At present no edition of this final pair of stories is in print, though doubtless they will reappear someday.

For obvious reasons, I cannot assess the virtues and faults of these tales. But they were heroic fantasy, or sword-and-sorcery fiction, long before these terms were coined. Robert E. Howard is rightly remembered as the American pioneer in this sub-genre, which had already been developed in Britain by William Morris, Lord Dunsany, and E. R. Eddison. Neither Pratt nor I, when we started the Harold Shea stories, had ever read a Conan tale or were familiar enough with Howard's work to know his name.

Pratt and I collaborated by meeting in Pratt's apartment and hammering out a plot by long discussion, while I took notes in shorthand, which I had taught myself. Back in my own quarters, I wrote a rough draft. Pratt then wrote a final draft, which I edited.

In a few cases, in our Gavagan's Bar short

fantasies, we reversed the procedure, Pratt doing the rough draft and I the final. This did not work out so well. In such collaborations, as I also found with other co-authors, it is generally better for the junior member to do the rough draft. He is likely to be more facile; while the senior member, by virtue of his greater experience, will probably have more skill at polishing and condensation and will be more alert for errors and inconsistencies.

In 1941, a colleague wrote an amusing fantasy novella for *Unknown*, "The Case of the Friendly Corpse." The hero has unintentionally swapped souls with an apprentice magician on another plane, who theretofore had been a student at the College of the Unholy Names. Another student tells the protagonist (now on this other plane) that Harold Shea appeared before him, claiming to be a magician from another world. The student challenged Harold: the student would turn his wand into a super-serpent. Harold would summon up his own monster, and they would see which creature won. But ". . . the snake just grew up and grabbed him and ate him before I could do anything about it."

Some readers were indignant at this brusque bumping off of a colleague's character. Pratt and I thought of writing a story to rescue Harold and turn the tables, but after some floundering we gave up. Another writer's *mise-en-scène*, we found, so hobbles the imagination that fancy plods when it ought to soar. In the end, we ignored our colleague's jape and sent Harold on to other *milieux*.

Pratt wrote over fifty books as well as many short stories, articles, and minor pieces. He wrote books on Napoleon, biographies of Edwin M. Stanton (Lincoln's Secretary of War) and King Valdemar IV of Denmark, a history of the U.S. Navy, and a couple of first-class heroic fantasies, *The Well of the Unicorn* and *The Blue Star*. He and I discussed further works of fiction, such as Harold Shea stories laid in the worlds of Persian and Indian myth. But they were never written.

In the 1950s, with the approach of the Civil War Centennial, Pratt was beginning to hit the best-seller lists with books on the Civil War. During this time, works on this conflict kept him too busy to have time for any fiction. Then, in 1956, at 59, he suddenly fell ill of cancer of the liver and soon died. Our mutual friend John D. Clark eventually married Pratt's widow.

I have been asked why I have not carried on the Harold Shea series alone. I have thought about it but have rejected the idea, at least for now. The main reason is that the combination of Pratt and de Camp produced a result rather different from the work of either of us alone. We complemented each other, because each of us knew a lot of things that the other did not, and Pratt knew much more about fictional techniques than I did. Collaboration is worthwhile when and only when each collaborator can furnish elements that the other lacks. Otherwise collaboration merely results in two people's each doing 75 percent of the work.

With my present experience, I could probably fake a Pratt–de Camp narrative pretty convincingly. But it would be a lot of hard work—I learned in my Conan pastiches how difficult it is to capture the intangible spirit of another's writings—and I have always had more ideas waiting to be reduced to writing than I could find time to get them all down.

When, however, I discovered that Tom and Bill had taken *The Tempest* as the setting for a Harold Shea adventure, I almost regretted my decision. What a perfect *milieu* for a Shea narrative! If I had thought of it first . . . Ah, well, perhaps it is just as well. In any case, I am sure you will enjoy the latest in the continuing saga of Harold's and Belphebe's desperate deeds in peculiar places.

> —L. Sprague de Camp
> Villanova, Pennsylvania
> September 1986

INTRODUCTION AND RULES TO CROSSROADS™ ADVENTURES
by Bill Fawcett

FOR THE MANY of us who have enjoyed the stories upon which this adventure is based, it may seem a bit strange to find an introduction this long at the start of a book. What you are holding is both a game and an adventure. Have you ever read a book and then told yourself you would have been able to think more clearly or seen a way out of the hero's dilemma? In a Crossroads™ adventure you have the opportunity to do just that. *You* make the key decisions. By means of a few easily followed steps you are able to see the results of your choices.

A Crossroads™ adventure is as much fun to read as it is to play. It is more than just a game or a book. It is a chance to enjoy once more a familiar and treasured story. The excitement of adventuring in a beloved universe is neatly blended into a story which stands well on its own merit, a story in which you will encounter many familiar characters and places and discover more than a few new ones as well. Each adventure is a thrilling tale, with the extra suspense and satisfaction of knowing that you will succeed or fail by your own endeavors.

THE ADVENTURE

Throughout the story you will have the opportunity to make decisions. Each of these decisions will affect whether the hero succeeds in the quest, or even survives. In some cases you will actually be fighting battles; other times you will use your knowledge and instincts to choose the best path to follow. In many cases there will be clues in the story or illustrations.

A Crossroads™ adventure is divided into sections. The length of a section may be a few lines or many pages. The section numbers are shown at the top of a page to make it easier for you to follow. Each section ends when you must make a decision, or fight. The next section you turn to will show the results of your decision. At least one six-sided die and a pencil are needed to "play" this book.

The words "six-sided dice" are often abbreviated as "D6." If more than one is needed, a number will precede the term. "Roll three six-sided dice" will be written as "Roll 3 D6." Virtually all the die rolls in these rules do involve rolling three six-sided dice (or rolling one six-sided die three times) and totaling what is rolled.

If you are an experienced role-play gamer, you may also wish to convert the values given in this novel to those you can use with your own fantasy campaign or any other role-playing game. All of the adventures have been constructed so that they also can be easily adapted in this manner. The values for the hero will transfer directly. While most games are much more complicated, doing this will allow you to be the Game Master for other players. Important values for the hero's opponents will be given to aid you in this conversion and to give those playing by the Crossroads™ rules a better idea of what they are facing.

THE HERO

Seven values are used to describe the hero in gaming terms. These are strength, intelligence, wisdom/luck, constitution, dexterity, charisma, and hit points. These values measure all of a character's abilities. At the end of these rules is a record sheet. On it are given all of the values for the hero of this adventure and any equipment or supplies they begin the adventure with. While you adventure, this record can be used to keep track of damage received and any new equipment or magical items acquired. You may find it advisable to make a photocopy of that page. Permission to do so, for your own use only, is given by the publisher of this game/novel. You may wish to consult this record sheet as we discuss what each of the values represents.

STRENGTH

This is the measure of how physically powerful your hero is. It compares the hero to others in how much the character can lift, how hard he can punch, and just how brawny he is. The strongest a normal human can be is to have a strength value of 18. The weakest a child would have is a 3. Here is a table giving comparable strengths:

Strength	Example
3	A 5-year-old child
6	An elderly man
8	Out of shape and over 40
10	An average 20-year-old man
13	In good shape and works out

15	A top athlete or football running back
17	Changes auto tires without a jack
18	Arm-wrestles Arnold Schwarzenegger and wins

A Tolkien-style troll, being magical, might have a strength of 19 or 20. A full-grown elephant has a strength of 23. A fifty-foot dragon would have a strength of 30.

INTELLIGENCE

Being intelligent is not just a measure of native brain power. It is also an indication of the ability to use that intelligence. The value for intelligence also measures how aware the character is, and so how likely they are to notice a subtle clue. Intelligence can be used to measure how resistant a mind is to hypnosis or mental attack. A really sharp baboon would have an intelligence of 3. Most humans (we all know exceptions) begin at about 5. The highest value possible is an 18. Here is a table of relative intelligence:

Intelligence	Example
3	My dog
5	Lassie

6	Curly (the third Stooge)
8	Somewhat slow
10	Average person
13	College professor/good quarterback
15	Indiana Jones/Carl Sagan
17	Doc Savage/Mr. Spock
18	Leonardo da Vinci (Isaac Asimov?)

Brainiac of comic-book fame would have a value of 21.

WISDOM/LUCK

Wisdom is the ability to make correct judgments, often with less than complete facts. Wisdom is knowing what to do and when to do it. Attacking, when running will earn you a spear in the back, is the best part of wisdom. Being in the right place at the right time can be called luck or wisdom. Not being discovered when hiding can be luck; if it is because you knew enough to not hide in the poison oak, wisdom is also a factor. Activities which are based more on instinct, the intuitive leap, than analysis are decided by wisdom.

In many ways both wisdom and luck are further connected, especially as wisdom also measures how friendly the ruling powers of the universe (not the author, the fates) are to the hero. A hero may be favored by fate or luck because he is reverent or for no discernible reason at all. This will give him a high wisdom value. Everyone knows those "lucky" individuals who can fall in the mud and find a gold coin. Here is a table measuring relative wisdom/luck:

Wisdom	Example
Under 3	Cursed or totally unthinking
5	Never plans, just reacts
7	Some cunning, "street smarts"
9	Average thinking person
11	Skillful planner, good gambler
13	Successful businessman/Lee Iacocca
15	Captain Kirk (wisdom)/Conan (luck)
17	Sherlock Holmes (wisdom)/Luke Skywalker (luck)
18	Lazarus Long

CONSTITUTION

The more you can endure, the higher your constitution. If you have a high constitution you are better able to survive physical damage, emotional stress, and poisons. The higher your value for constitution, the longer you are able to continue functioning in a difficult situation. A character with a high constitution can run farther (though not necessarily faster) or hang by one hand longer than the average person. A high constitution means you also have more stamina, and recover more quickly from injuries. A comparison of values for constitution:

Constitution	Example
3	A terminal invalid
6	A 10-year-old child
8	Your stereotyped "98-pound weakling"
10	Average person
14	Olympic athlete/Sam Spade
16	Marathon runner/Rocky
18	Rasputin/Batman

A whale would have a constitution of 20. Superman's must be about 50.

DEXTERITY

The value for dexterity measures not only how fast a character can move, but how well-coordinated those movements are. A surgeon, a pianist, and a juggler all need a high value for dexterity. If you have a high value for dexterity you can react quickly (though not necessarily correctly), duck well, and perform sleight-of-hand magic (if you are bright enough to learn how). Conversely, a low dexterity means you react slowly and drop things frequently. All other things being equal, the character with the highest dexterity will have the advantage of the first attack in a combat. Here are some comparative examples of dexterity:

Dexterity	Example
3 or less	Complete klutz
5	Inspector Clouseau
6	Can walk and chew gum, most of the time
8	Barney Fife
10	Average person
13	Good fencer/Walter Payton
15	Brain surgeon/Houdini
16	Flying Karamazov Brothers
17	Movie ninja/Cyrano de Bergerac
18	Bruce Lee

Batman, Robin, Daredevil, and The Shadow all have a dexterity of 19. At a dexterity of 20 you don't even see the man move before he has taken your wallet and underwear and has left the room (the Waco Kid).

CHARISMA

Charisma is more than just good looks, though they certainly don't hurt. It is a measure of how persuasive a hero is and how willing others are to do what he wants. You can have average looks yet be very persuasive, and have a high charisma. If your value for charisma is high, you are better able to talk yourself out of trouble or obtain information from a stranger. If your charisma is low, you may be ignored or even mocked, even when you are right. A high charisma value is vital to entertainers of any sort, and leaders. A different type of charisma is just as important to spies. In the final measure a high value for charisma means people will react to you in the way you desire. Here are some comparative values for charisma:

Charisma	Example
3	Hunchback of Notre Dame
5	An ugly used-car salesman
7	Richard Nixon today
10	Average person
12	Team coach

14	Magnum, P.I.
16	Henry Kissinger/Jim DiGriz
18	Dr. Who/Prof. Harold Hill (Centauri)

HIT POINTS

Hit points represent the total amount of damage a hero can take before he is killed or knocked out. You can receive damage from being wounded in a battle, through starvation, or even through a mental attack. Hit points measure more than just how many times the hero can be battered over the head before he is knocked out. They also represent the ability to keep striving toward a goal. A poorly paid mercenary may have only a few hit points, even though he is a hulking brute of a man, because the first time he receives even a slight wound he will withdraw from the fight. A blacksmith's apprentice who won't accept defeat will have a higher number of hit points.

A character's hit points can be lost through a wound to a specific part of the body or through general damage to the body itself. This general damage can be caused by a poison, a bad fall, or even exhaustion and starvation. Pushing your body too far beyond its limits may result in a successful action at the price of the loss of a few hit points. All these losses are treated in the same manner.

Hit points lost are subtracted from the total on the hero's record sheet. When a hero has lost all of his hit points, then that character has failed. When this happens you will be told to which section to turn. Here you will often find a description of the failure and its consequences for the hero.

The hit points for the opponents the hero meets in combat are given in the adventure. You should keep track of these hit points on a piece of scrap paper. When a monster or opponent has lost all of their hit points, they have lost the fight. If a character is fighting more than one opponent, then you should keep track of each of their hit points. Each will continue to fight until it has 0 hit points. When everyone on one side of the battle has no hit points left, the combat is over.

Even the best played character can lose all of his hit points when you roll too many bad dice during a combat. If the hero loses all of his hit points, the adventure may have ended in failure. You will be told so in the next section you are instructed to turn to. In this case you can turn back to the first section and begin again. This time you will have the advantage of having learned some of the hazards the hero will face.

TAKING CHANCES

There will be occasions where you will have to decide whether the hero should attempt to perform some action which involves risk. This might be to climb a steep cliff, jump a pit, or juggle three daggers. There will be other cases where it might benefit the hero to notice something subtle or remember an ancient ballad perfectly. In all of these cases you will be asked to roll three six-sided dice (3 D6) and compare the total of all three dice to the hero's value for the appropriate ability.

For example, if the hero is attempting to juggle three balls, then for him to do so successfully you would have to roll a total equal to or less than the hero's value for dexterity. If your total was less than this dexterity value, then you would be directed to a section describing how the balls looked as they were skillfully juggled. If you rolled a higher value than that for dexterity, then you would be told to read a section which describes the embarrassment of dropping the balls, and being laughed at by the audience.

Where the decision is a judgment call, such as whether to take the left or right staircase, it is left entirely to you. Somewhere in the adventure or in the original novels there will be some piece of information which would indicate that the left staircase leads to a trap and the right to your goal. No die roll will be needed for a judgment decision.

In all cases you will be guided at the end of each section as to exactly what you need do. If you have any questions you should refer back to these rules.

MAGICAL ITEMS AND SPECIAL EQUIPMENT

There are many unusual items which appear in the pages of this adventure. When it is possible for them to be taken by the hero, you will be given the option of doing so. One or more of these items may be necessary to the successful completion of the adventure. You will be given the option of taking these at the end of a section. If you choose to pick up an item and succeed in getting it, you should list that item on the hero's record sheet. There is no guarantee that deciding to take an item means you will actually obtain it. If someone owns it already they are quite likely to resent your efforts to take it. In some cases things may not even be all they appear to be or the item may be trapped or cursed. Having it may prove a detriment rather than a benefit.

All magical items give the hero a bonus (or penalty) on certain die rolls. You will be told when this applies, and often given the option of whether or not to use the item. You will be instructed at the end of the section on how many points to add to or subtract from your die roll. If you choose to use an item which can function only once, such as a magic potion or hand grenade, then you will also be instructed to remove the item from your record sheet. Certain items, such as a magic sword, can be used many times. In this case you will be told when you obtain the item when you can apply the bonus. The bonus for a magic sword could be added every time a character is in hand-to-hand combat.

Other special items may allow a character to fly, walk through fire, summon magical warriors, or many other things. How and when they affect play will again be told to you in the paragraphs at the end of the sections where you have the choice of using them.

Those things which restore lost hit points are a special case. You may choose to use these at any time during the adventure. If you have a magical healing potion which returns 1 D6 of lost hit points, you may add these points when you think it is best to. This can even be during a combat in the place of a round of attack. No matter how many healing items you use, a character can never have more hit points than he begins the adventure with.

There is a limit to the number of special items any character may carry. In any Crossroads™ adventure the limit is four items. If you already have four special items listed on your record sheet, then one of these must be discarded in order to take the new item. Any time you erase an item off the record sheet, whether because it was used or because you wish to add a new item, whatever is erased is permanently lost. It can never be "found" again, even if you return to the same location later in the adventure.

Except for items which restore hit points, the hero can only use an item in combat or when given the option to do so. The opportunity will be listed in the instructions.

In the case of an item which can be used in every combat, the bonus can be added or subtracted as the description of the item indicates. A +2 sword would add two points to any total rolled in combat. This bonus would be used each and every time the hero attacks. Only one attack bonus can be used at a time. Just because a hero has both a +1 and a +2 sword doesn't mean he knows how to fight with both at once. Only the better bonus would apply.

If a total of 12 is needed to hit an attacking monster and the hero has a +2 sword, then you will only need to roll a total of 10 on the three dice to successfully strike the creature.

You could also find an item, perhaps enchanted armor, which could be worn in all combat and would have the effect of subtracting its bonus from the total of any opponent's attack on its wearer. (Bad guys can wear magic armor, too.) If a monster normally would need a 13 to hit a character who has obtained a set of +2 armor, then the monster would now need a total of 15 to score a hit. An enchanted shield would operate in the same way, but could never be used when the character was using a weapon which needed both hands, such as a pike, longbow, or two-handed sword.

COMBAT

There will be many situations where the hero will be forced, or you may choose, to meet an opponent in combat. The opponents can vary from a wild beast, to a human thief, or an unearthly monster. In all cases the same steps are followed.

The hero will attack first in most combats unless you are told otherwise. This may happen when there is an ambush, other special situations, or because the opponent simply has a much higher dexterity.

At the beginning of a combat section you will be given the name or type of opponent involved. For each combat five values are given. The first of these is the total on three six-sided dice needed for the attacker to hit the hero. Next to this value is the value the hero needs to hit these opponents. After these two values is listed the hit points of the opponent. If there is more than one opponent, each one will have the same number. (See the Hit Points section included earlier if you are unclear as to what these do.) Under the value needed to be hit by the opponent is the hit points of damage that it will do to the hero when it attacks successfully. Finally, under the total needed for the hero to successfully hit an opponent is the damage he will do with the different weapons he might have. Unlike a check for completing a daring action (where you wish to roll under a value), in a combat you have to roll the value given or higher on three six-sided dice to successfully hit an opponent.

For example:

Here is how a combat between the hero armed with a sword and three brigands armed only with daggers is written:

BRIGANDS
To hit the hero: 14   To be hit: 12   Hit points: 4
Damage with   Damage with
daggers: 1 D6   sword: 2 D6
(used by the   (used by the
brigands)   hero)
There are three brigands. If two are killed

(taken to 0 hit points) the third will flee in panic.

If the hero wins, turn to section 85.

If he is defeated, turn to section 67.

RUNNING AWAY

Running rather than fighting, while often desirable, is not always possible. The option to run away is available only when listed in the choices. Even when this option is given, there is no guarantee the hero can get away safely.

THE COMBAT SEQUENCE

Any combat is divided into alternating rounds. In most cases the hero will attack first. Next, surviving opponents will have the chance to fight back. When both have attacked, one round will have been completed. A combat can have any number of rounds and continues until the hero or his opponents are defeated. Each round is the equivalent of six seconds. During this time all the parties in the combat may actually take more than one swing at each other.

The steps in resolving a combat in which the hero attacks first are as follows:

1. Roll three six-sided dice. Total the numbers showing on all three and add any bonuses from weapons or special circumstances. If this total is the same or greater than the second value given, "to hit the opponent," then the hero has successfully attacked.

2. If the hero attacks successfully, the next step is to determine how many hit points of damage he did to the opponent. The die roll for this will be given below the "to hit opponent" information.

3. Subtract any hit points of damage done from the opponent's total.

4. If any of the enemy have one or more hit points left, then the remaining opponent or opponents now can attack. Roll three six-sided dice for each attacker. Add up each of these sets of three dice. If the total is the same as or greater than the value listed after "to hit the hero" in the section describing the combat, the attack was successful.

5. For each hit, roll the number of dice listed for damage. Subtract the total from the number of hit points the hero has at that time. Enter the new, lower total on the hero's record sheet.

If both the hero and one or more opponents have hit points left, the combat continues. Start again at step one. The battle ends only when the hero is killed, all the opponents are killed, or all of one side has run away. A hero cannot, except through a healing potion or spells or when specifically told to during the adventure, regain lost hit points. A number of small wounds from several opponents will kill a character as thoroughly as one titanic, unsuccessful combat with a hill giant.

DAMAGE

The combat continues, following the sequence given below, until either the hero or his opponents have no hit points. In the case of multiple opponents, subtract hit points from one opponent until the total reaches 0 or less. Extra hit points of damage done on the round when each opponent is defeated are lost. They do not carry over to the next enemy in the group. To win the combat, you must eliminate all of an opponent's hit points.

The damage done by a weapon will vary depending on who is using it. A club in the hands of a child will do far less damage than the same club wielded by a hill giant. The maximum damage is given as a number of six-sided dice. In some cases the maximum will be less than a whole die. This is abbreviated by a minus sign followed by a number. For example, D6−2, meaning one roll of a six-sided die, minus two. The total damage can never be less than zero, meaning no damage done. 2 D6−1 means that you should roll two six-sided dice and then subtract one from the total of them both.

A combat may, because of the opponent involved, have one or more special circumstances. It may be that the enemy will surrender or flee when its hit point total falls below a certain level, or even that reinforcements will arrive to help the bad guys after so many rounds. You will be told of these special situations in the lines directly under the combat values.

Now you may turn to section 1.

RECORD SHEET

Harold Shea

Strength	11	Hit Points	17
Intelligence	14		
Wisdom	11	Magical Items	
Constitution	13	1.	
Dexterity	15	2.	
Charisma	3	3.	
		4.	

Items carried: cigarette lighter, pocket knife

Section 1

* 1 *

"Well, Doc, I'm ready for your lecture," Vaclav Polacek says as he strolls into the room. "You know, the one on magic. If I'm gonna be coming and going between parallel universes, I gotta be a good magician."

"It would help a lot, Votsy, if you could do something besides turn yourself into a werewolf every time there's trouble," mutters Harold Shea as he shifts in his chair.

"Gentlemen," interrupts the bushy-haired man behind the desk. "I'm in . . . uh . . . full agreement with Vaclav. It wouldn't hurt any of us to study the principles of 'magic' for they are, in reality, the physics of other universes. From my long stay in Faerie and that abortive trip to the Furioso, I believe I finally have a grasp of the measurable qualities of the fourth, fifth, and sixth dimensions. So, beginning tomorrow at this time, we shall commence daily discussions on the subject. There has got to be . . . uh . . . more *method* to our madness."

The man speaking is Reed Chalmers, once director of psychologists at the Garaden Institute, now in charge of the hush-hush "Interplanar Project." He has just returned

Section 1

from a rather protracted stay in two different parallel universes. Gathered around him are the new director of psychology, Walter Bayard, and two psychologists, the outspoken Vaclav Polacek and Harold Shea. The fifth man in the room is the most unlikely member of the group, a recently retired police detective named Pete Brodsky.

"As you know," Chalmers continues, "ever since Harold here proved that our—uh—'syllogismobile' actually works, we've been involved in a series of willy-nilly chases from one universe to another . . . often narrowly escaping with our lives."

"I can't say that I found my stay in Xanadu either unpleasant or dangerous," puts in a sleepy-eyed Bayard.

"That's beside the point, Walter," answers Chalmers. "I never should have dragged you, Polacek, and Brodsky into that affair in the first place. It's a perfect example of imperfect science. We have to be aware of the disturbance that our various disappearances have caused here at the Institute. Our recent brush with the police is something we dare not repeat."

"No need to thank me, boys, for squaring things between you guys and the law," Brodsky says, smiling broadly.

"So, it's time we started minding our extra-dimensional P's and Q's, eh, Doc?" says Polacek.

Section 1

Chalmers leans forward in his chair. "We've done enough swashbuckling . . . and I'm afraid I must personally bear a large portion of the responsibility. But no more! Now we begin the application of serious and ordered scientific method. And since we're all back here safely in Ohio, there must be no more trips until we analyze the data we now possess."

"That's fine for you, Dr. Chalmers," Bayard says with annoyance, "you and Harold married dream girls you brought back from the land of Faerie. My Dunyazad was sent back to Xanadu quite without my consent. What about the rest of us?"

Shea remembers that Walter was actually quite relieved when the houri was accidentally sent back and wonders what Bayard is really complaining about.

"Seems to me, you guys have got something here that's too hot to handle," says Brodsky. "If word of this gets out, every Tom, Dick, and Harry is gonna want to go off to the world of his dreams."

"Precisely the problem!" answers Chalmers. He turns to Bayard. "Walter, I'm not closing the door to the rest of you, I merely want a temporary halt to inter-dimensional travel. We're sitting on the greatest cosmological discovery in history. We must be very, very careful until we are ready to publish our findings."

Section 1

Chalmers stands up, resting his hands on his desk. "Then we all agree. No more trips will be made into parallel universes until further notice." He looks around the room and peers seriously into each man's eyes.

Polacek, who has stopped in a corner, resumes his pacing and opens his mouth to speak. Reed Chalmers continues, "I want all of you, including Brodsky here, to prepare written reports on your recent—uh—experiences." There is a general groan from those present. "I want you to note every detail about the acts of magic you saw or experienced. We must leave no stone unturned. We must determine exactly what we have done to transport ourselves and others to parallel worlds. Our formulae must be refined and made more accurate."

"Not to mention the fact, Doc, that we've never once gotten back without help from the locals," adds Shea.

There is a murmur of agreement. Chalmers goes on, "Vaclav, I'm putting you in charge of correlating our experiences with the magic or, more accurately, the physics of the various worlds we have visited . . . with my assistance and guidance, of course." The Czech beams with obvious pleasure.

"Don't look so smug, Votsy," interrupts Shea. "The only way we'll ever be able to trust you with magic is to make you an expert on the subject."

Section 1

The Rubber Czech shoots Harold an evil glance as Reed Chalmers closes the meeting. "Yes, well then, I think that will be enough for today. And remember, gentlemen, be careful what you say, and *no* experimenting on your own."

Harold Shea stops typing and leans back in his chair. Two weeks have passed since Doc Chalmers asked for the reports, and Harold has still not finished his. Of course, some of his experiences are over a year old. His eyes drift across the room to his wife, Belphebe. She is seated at a table in the den, busily fletching arrows for her bow. Not everybody, he thinks to himself, can be married to a red-haired, freckle-faced huntress. The main problem with being married to a huntress from the woods of Faerie is that she is not too happy living in the city as the wife of a modern American psychologist.

He has solved part of the problem by moving them out of his town house. Together, they picked out a lovely place in the woods at the edge of town. It isn't perfect . . . their backyard is a giant cornfield. But oaks and maples border them on two sides.

Harold and Belphebe have made a pact. If it isn't raining, they sleep outside in the trees on even-numbered days. Otherwise, she joins him in the bedroom. He looks out the window into the gray drizzle and smiles. It

Section 1

has rained every day since they moved in.

He stares down at the page in his typewriter and his mind drifts back to his last adventure. He was in Ireland with the Sidhe of Connacht. His conversations with the Druid Miach seemed to explain a lot. "Ye canna be released from a wurrld without accomplishing something ta alter the pattern o' the wurrld itself." Is this Harold Shea's personal geas, or does it apply to all of those from the Institute who have traveled to another continuum? He makes a mental note to discuss this concept with Doc Chalmers.

The clock in the hall chimes six, and Shea is startled to see Belphebe standing before him.

"Harold, darling, is it not time we were leaving for this place you call the theater? Sir Reed and Lady Florimel will be awaiting."

"What . . . oh, of course, dear," answers Shea. "Just give me a minute to change. You *are* going to wear the long green dress, aren't you?"

"If you insist," his wife says reluctantly.

"I insist!" After he lost her favorite dress in the frozen wastes of the Finnish Kalevala, she reluctantly accepted his gifts of twentieth-century clothing. Tonight is a special occasion. The psychologists were given complimentary tickets to a Shakespeare festival, and Harold already picked out a lovely

Section 1

formal dress and matching high-heeled shoes for Belphebe to wear.

"And I will drive," she states flatly.

He hesitates. "Uh . . . yes, dearest." Belphebe at the wheel of their Chevrolet is an experience that requires nerves of steel. But she has agreed to wear the dress.

The first act of *The Tempest* has come to an end. Harold stands in the crowded lobby talking to Reed Chalmers.

"Y'know, Doc, I hadn't really thought much about it before, but the world described in this play looks like a target for our explorations."

Chalmers frowns. "If it were based more on myth and legend, I would agree with you, but I do not believe it to be a systematically attainable universe. Shakespeare drew his material from a confusion of Greek and Roman mythology, sixteenth-century Italian pastoral drama, and God knows what else."

"Think a minute, Doc. Spenser's *Faerie Queene* is the same sort of thing. It was based on Ariosto's *Orlando Furioso*, and we managed to travel to both places." Shea senses that he has won his point and smiles. "A trip to Prospero's magical Mediterranean island shouldn't be difficult. It may be a Shakespearean romance, but it describes a valid parallel universe."

Section 1

"That, I am afraid, is what is worrying me, Harold. I'm sure it would be possible. Ever since Vaclav and I beat our hasty retreat from that irate husband in the Furioso, he's been dropping little hints. I think he might be up to something. Did you notice what he is wearing tonight?"

"Is Vaclav here?" asks Shea.

"Indeed! Sitting two rows behind you. He's dressed as a fourteenth-century Italian courtier. We must have a talk with him."

Shea nods in agreement. Polacek found his dream girl in the world of Orlando Furioso, all right. True to form, however, the Czech found two of them. And one of them has a jealous innkeeper for a husband.

Just then the lights dim, and Florimel and Belphebe appear before them, stunning in their strapless gowns. The matter of Vaclav Polacek and his fourteenth-century garb would have to wait.

When they reach their seats, Shea turns to look at the audience. Almost directly behind him, dressed in a gaudy orange silk jacket with puffy brown shoulder pads, sits the Czech. Vaclav notices him, nods, and smiles pleasantly. Harold isn't sure he likes that smile.

The play resumes, and Shea allows himself to become immersed in the trials and tribulations of the shipwrecked King of Naples. Alonso is just saying "Prithee peace" for the second time when the hairs on the back of Shea's neck begin to tingle.

Belphebe tugs at his arm and whispers, "My, how this play does excite me."

Harold begins to worry. The play isn't that exciting, and he has felt this way before.... Vaclav! Shea cranes his neck to get a look at Polacek, but even as he turns, the crowd around him begins to fade to a foggy gray. Desperately, he grabs Belphebe's hand and—

PMF!

Harold and Belphebe plop to the ground in a field of green grass.

"Oof!" cries his wife as she lands. Shea looks around. They are in a green field surrounded by low, tree-covered hills. A fresh breeze hits him in the face. He shakes his head in disbelief. The characters in the play had just been talking about this place.

"Shea, Belphebe!" cries a distressed voice from behind them. "What are you guys doing here? I—I had no idea...."

Harold climbs to his feet. There, sprawled in the grass, is Vaclav Polacek in his ludicrous costume.

"Votsy, I'm going to kill you!" Shea bellows with murder in his eyes. "You've dragged us into the play!" He starts ominously toward the Czech.

"Honest, Harold, I didn't mean to bring you two along...." Polacek tries to scram-

Section 1

ble to his feet, but Shea is on him in a flash, and the unfortunate Czech is wrestled to the ground.

"Gik, you're choking me!" gurgles Polacek.

"If you possessed even half a brain!" rages Shea, "you'd have trouble . . ."

Belphebe intervenes, pulling her husband off the bluish psychologist. "Vaclav, Harold! Stop this foolishness. Have you not better things to do than fight among yourselves?"

The Czech sits up, rubbing his neck. "I really meant to come alone, honest!"

"It's that damn magicostatic charge," fumes Shea. "Belphebe and I are heavily charged. When you transported yourself here, you pulled us along with you. Doc Chalmers is lucky he wasn't sitting as close to you as we were."

Polacek picks up a book he dropped, brushes himself off, and stands up, regarding Shea with a cautious gaze.

Shea continues, "So what's the big idea, Votsy? You know the Doc doesn't want us doing this until he's got it perfected."

"Look," answers the Czech, "I just figured I'd jump in here, grab the old man's daughter and some of his magic books, and then beat it back to Ohio."

"Now that's a hell of a fine plan!" says Shea in disgust. "This guy Prospero is one powerful magician, and he's got invisible

Section 1

spirits to help him. Just how did you propose to kidnap his daughter and steal his library?"

"Hey, gimme some credit. While you guys were writing reports, I've been busy studying this magic business pretty seriously." Polacek holds up the book. "This here is the Doc's latest symbolic magic textbook." He thumbs through several pages. "And I can still read the symbols in this continuum."

"That's all well and good, Votsy, but that book is full of untried theory as far as this place is concerned," grumbles Shea.

"All right already," answers Vaclav. "Hows about I send you and the missus back to Ohio?" He begins flipping pages.

Harold recalls his geas and sighs. "It's no good, Votsy. We have to alter this place before we can leave."

"Nonsense." Vaclav nudges Belphebe closer to Shea. "You two hold hands and think Ohio thoughts." Belphebe does so and Polacek begins motioning in the air with his free hand. "If either A or (B or C) is true, and C . . ."

"Wait a minute!" yells Shea angrily. "Even if this would work, which it won't, I'm not leaving you here alone." He looks off into the hills. "Besides, we don't even know where we are. For all we know we could be back in the land of Faerie."

Belphebe speaks: "Nay, Harold, 'tis not

Section 1

Faerie. We are indeed in a strange land, methinks the very one spoken of in the play." Suddenly she points up into the sky. "Look, there!"

Shea and Polacek gaze skyward but can see nothing.

"'Tis some sort of creature slowly circling," she continues.

"Damn! We better find some cover," says Shea, "before that spirit Ariel reports us to Prospero. I don't think we'll be too welcome here." They hurry across the field, heading for the nearest trees.

Belphebe stumbles, catching her heel in a clump of grass. "These do me no good in this place." She takes off her high heels and is about to toss them away.

"Better keep those, dear," says Shea. "Even if you can't wear them, they're still high fashion. Maybe Miranda will like them." Actually, he is remembering just how much he paid for those shoes only the day before. Belphebe shoots him an angry look and continues barefoot, holding the offending shoes in her hand.

They soon come to a little stream and splash across to a grove of trees on the far side. They then work their way upstream to where the sparse timber gives way to dense forest.

At length, Shea sits down on a rock. "Well, whatever that was in the sky must not have

Section 1

seen us. Let's stop a moment and take stock of our situation. Votsy, did you bring anything besides the book?"

The Czech rummages through his pockets and looks up rather sheepishly. "Sorry," he admits. "Nothing but a pocketful of change, keys, and my wallet."

Shea looks at his wife. "Anything useful in your purse?" he asks. She frowns and dumps out a small pile of assorted cosmetics. He begins to wish he hadn't tried quite so hard to convert her to twentieth-century fashion.

"Well, that's just great," Shea says heavily as he searches through his suit and produces a cigarette lighter and a pocket knife. "As you can see, we are well equipped for life in the wild."

Belphebe grabs the knife. "With this I can fashion a bow and arrows, though 'tis a shame that I left such a fine one not long ago in our house." She darts off into the woods.

"Say, Harold," says Vaclav, "you wouldn't happen to have a cigarette to go with that lighter, would you?"

Shea pulls a pack out of his breast pocket and tosses it to the Czech. "Here, have fun."

Polacek puts a cigarette in his mouth and flips open the top of the lighter.

"You realize," says Shea with a cynical smile, "that thing won't work here. Remember how Brodsky's gun wouldn't fire in Xanadu."

Section 1

Vaclav calmly flips the wheel and produces a flame. Shea stares in amazement, then grabs the lighter and tries it himself. Again there is fire. He remembers how his matches wouldn't work when he had tried to light a fire for Thor and Loki.

"Looks like some of our physical principles apply to this world," says Polacek. "At least flint and steel can make butane burn." He blows a puff of smoke into the air.

"Or maybe we're still somewhere in the U.S.A. Hand me that book and I'll try some magic," says Shea.

"Oh, no you don't!" Vaclav yells defensively. "I've been studying the art, you know. I'll do the magicking." He thinks for a moment. "How about I summon up some chow?"

Shea grimaces in disgust and reluctantly agrees. Two weeks with Reed Chalmers isn't enough training.

Harold goes to work gathering small twigs. Meanwhile, the Czech searches the nearby trees until he finds a small blue caterpillar. He carefully builds a framework of the twigs and places the insect on top of it. Shea wonders just what kind of meal can be made from a blue caterpillar and then decides that he really doesn't want to know.

Polacek begins waving his hands in the air. Then he recites:

Section 1

"I've never seen a purple cow.
I've never hoped to see one.
But I can tell you anyhow!
I'd rather see than be one!"

Horrified, Shea yells, "No! Stop!" but it is too late. A sudden rush of air followed by a dense cloud of purple smoke rises from the caterpillar. The smoke stings Shea's eyes. He rubs them, and when he opens them, Vaclav Polacek is gone.

There, standing before Shea, is an immense, sad-eyed purple cow. It moos plaintively and begins munching some grass by the edge of the stream.

"Well, Votsy, at least you proved that we're not in Ohio. And, I might add, I'm not sure that I can change you back." The cow moans and rolls its eyes. "It takes time to learn the nuances of the magic in the worlds we enter." Shea leans over and picks the book up from under the purple cow.

He still prefers the cards he made for his last set of adventures, but the book does have certain advantages, if it can be read. He studies the logic symbols. In this continuum, he is unable to read the notes scribbled in English around the edge of the page, but the pictograms show how to summon a medium-sized animal. Since he can no longer read English, he wonders just what language they are speaking here.

Section 1

Probably a mixture of Italian and Middle English.

Suddenly, a sinister laugh seems to float out of the treetops behind him. Shea turns to look but can see nothing unusual. The laugh comes again, this time from a bush across the stream. Once again, he sees nothing.

"Hee, hee, hee," cackles the mysterious voice, this time originating from behind the purple cow, which is now calmly munching the underbrush.

"Who's there?" calls Shea as he looks around desperately for something he can use as a weapon. He spots a fallen branch, grabs it, and begins snapping off the twigs. Not much defense, he thinks, but better than nothing. The laugh comes again, from behind the tree next to him. Shea lifts his makeshift staff.

"Some minister of magicks thou art," says the voice. "Would'st thou change thyself into such a beast too?" The air in front of Shea begins to blur and ripple. In a flash an enormous, birdlike creature appears before him. Its wings beat noisily back and forth stirring up leaves, but its head is that of a dark-haired woman. The entire creature is frazzled and dirty.

It rises into the air and hovers above Shea, extending an enormous clawed talon. "I'll thank thee for that volume," shrieks the creature. "My mistress would have it on her

Section 1

shelf." The purple cow lets out a baleful moan and trots off into the woods.

Remove the pocket knife from Shea's list of possessions.

If Shea tries to fight the harpy, turn to section 33.

If Shea tries to run away, turn to section 51.

Section 2

* 2 *

Shea nods in agreement. "Belphebe," he says softly, "you cover us. We'll wait till they get to that dead tree. Snag, you go around to the right and stay low. I'll come at them from behind. Votsy!" Shea hisses. The Czech is still chowing down. "Get up here. You're gonna be the bait."

"What?" complains Polacek as he finishes a bottle of wine. Snag reaches over and grabs the Czech by his collar, lifts him bodily, and stands him up behind the rock.

Shea continues, pointing out the approaching goblins, "When those guys reach that tree, I want you to rush at them. And make a lot of noise."

"But what if they . . ."

Belphebe brandishes her bow. "Fear not, Vaclav," she says reassuringly, "they'll be dead before they can hurt you."

"Don't kill them both," says Shea. "I want a prisoner!"

Snag has already disappeared down the hillside as Shea circles behind a clump of tall thornbushes. He crosses a gully on a fallen log and loses sight of the goblins. Just then he hears Polacek screaming, followed by

Section 2

several thumps and the twunk of Belphebe's arrow. By the time Shea arrives, one goblin lies dead, and Snag is sitting on top of the other, holding its own club across its neck.

Polacek is sitting down, holding his head in his hands and moaning. "Where were you?" he asks, seeing Shea walk up.

"T'would seem our dead foe struck Vaclav a blow!" says Snag rather cheerfully. "And now I would throttle the other!" He mashes the club down on the goblin's neck, and its yellow eyes bulge as it makes choking sounds.

Belphebe arrives silently, and the goblin is tied to a tree. It sullenly refuses to talk until Snag puts a knife to its stomach and threatens to disembowel it slowly. The goblin quickly tells of an entrance used only by "employees" that is usually left unguarded. Belphebe manages to keep Snag from killing the hapless goblin, and they leave it firmly tied to the tree.

The brooms are stashed under a clump of brown bushes on top of the hill. Harold persuades Belphebe to leave her longbow as well, as it is unsuited for quick travel in the tight passages of a cave. The storm has abated, though it still drizzles as they make their way in the gathering dusk of evening. The entrance to the cave is hidden at the end of a steep valley behind the hill. After a brief discussion, Polacek happily agrees to stand

Section 2

guard at the exit with Snag, while Shea and Belphebe go in to steal the magic book.

"What do we do if you guys don't come out?" asks the Czech.

"We rescue them," Snag says curtly.

"My thoughts, exactly," adds Shea. "Give us till morning, then do something if we're not back."

Belphebe leads the way to the low entrance where they find a convenient supply of crude torches. Shea's lighter provides fire, and they set off into the cool darkness. At first the going is easy, as the floor consists of firmly packed clay. There is little sign of use, and they see only the occasional goblin footprint. The tunnel suddenly narrows and then merges with a much larger passage. They turn right and continue downhill.

Turn to section 6.

Section 3

* **3** *

Shea picks his way through the disgusting tangle of thornbushes as best he can and heads northeast. Occasionally he catches glimpses of the trail and goblin travelers, but soon he can no longer see them, even when he climbs into a dead tree at the top of a high hill. By now the sky is glowing red with twilight, and if Shea wasn't tired, hungry, and lost in a strange land, he probably would have enjoyed the sight. He thinks wistfully of Belphebe and hopes she is safe. He mutters a vow that he will find her.

Soon it is too dark to continue. Shea stops wearily and picks up a small stick. Maybe he can cast a light spell upon it so he will have enough light to continue. He spends several frustrating minutes mumbling all sorts of incantations, but none of them rhymes very well and, what is worse, none of them works. He throws the stick away in anger and decides to make another flying broom but, try as he might, he cannot find a bird feather in this desolate place. Night comes on, and a thoroughly discouraged Harold Shea begins to clear a sleeping area.

He has just settled down to an uncomfort-

Section 3

able night's rest with a rock poking him in the side when a flash of light suddenly catches his eye. He shakes his head and looks again and spots a familiar, glowing red ball atop the next hill. It is circling slowly. A fairy!

Shea stumbles rapidly up the hill. When he reaches the summit, the red fairy buzzes excitedly around his head and then starts off into the dark. Shea follows. The fairy leads him along a rough path. After climbing what seems like an endless procession of low hills, Shea is rewarded by the sight of several fairies circling in the darkness.

Turn to section 61.

Section 4

* 4 *

A hail of large stones whiz overhead, and Shea throws himself to the ground just in the nick of time. A group of sailors nearly runs over him as they charge forward brandishing homemade spears. Shea dashes over to a dead tree, hurriedly gathers some twigs, and then runs over to the beach. Oblivious to the din of battle, he begins shaping little forms out of the wet sand and places two twigs in the nose of each figure. They don't look much like rhinoceroses, but there is no time to lose.

There is a tremendous crash of thunder, and Shea looks up to see the left flank of the sailor army enveloped in flames. He glances around anxiously until he sees Belphebe and her entourage of archers, still holding their ground. Shea stands back and begins making passes over his tiny models, chanting rapidly:

> "O creatures who feed,
>   On dank jungle's weed,
> Rise up from the sand!
>   And heed my demand . . ."

Shea ducks as a long black spear whizzes past his left ear. He resumes:

Section 4

"With tempers most foul,
   And anger in bowel,
Come out of the jungle with your double
   horn,
   I conjure you all now, arise and be
      born!"

The little images begin to blur and a fine spray of sand is thrown up into the air around him. Shea curses to himself, he has forgotten to invoke a deity... yet something is happening. He looks over to Belphebe, who stopped to watch him. Her jaw drops open. Just then, something large, brown, cold, and slimy slaps him in the face and throws him to the sand.

Shea struggles to his knees and is shocked to see himself surrounded by a herd of enormous twenty-foot lizards, each one with two silly-looking horns sticking out of its nose. They begin to waddle awkwardly off into the midst of the battle, looking something like the dinosaurs in a low-budget Hollywood movie. Oh well, thinks Shea, not exactly rhinos, but they look pretty fearsome.

He runs back to Belphebe's side.

"Marry, Harold, but those are the strangest creatures you have yet summoned," she says calmly as she lets loose her last arrow at an advancing goblin. Already the witch's

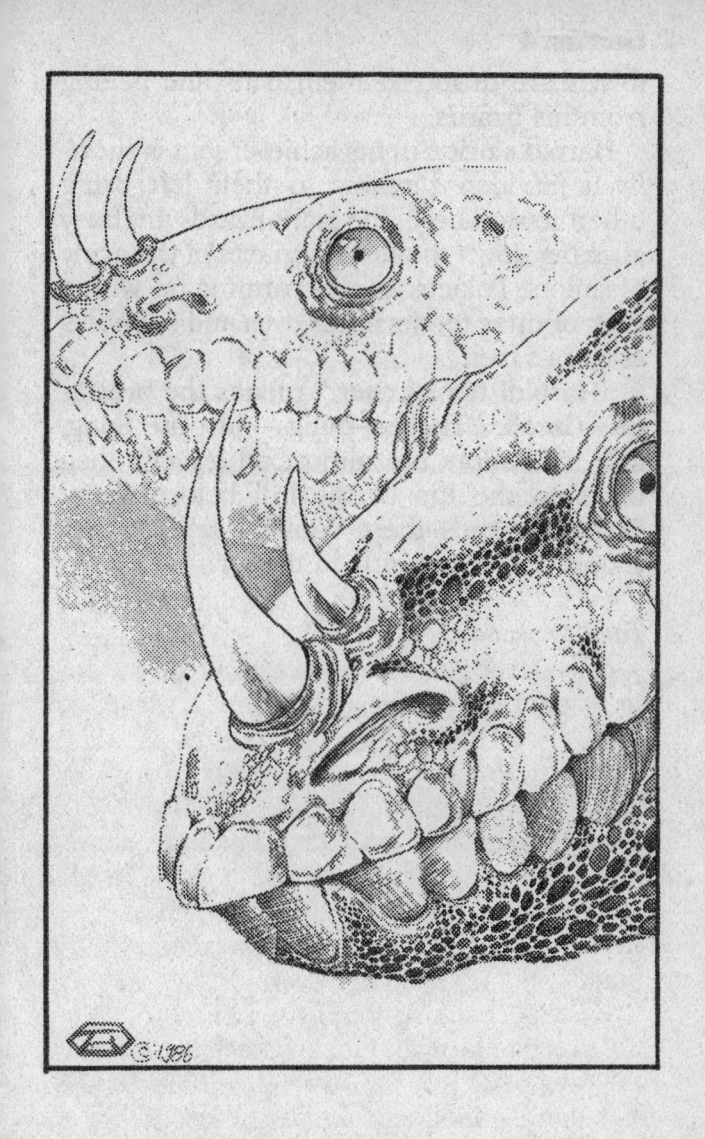
©1986

Section 4

forces are dropping their arms and fleeing from his lizards.

Harold's pride in his achievement is short-lived. Sudden screams to their left bring other news. There, the giant lizards are busy choking down the last remnants of the army of sailors. Polacek comes running up with a look of utter terror in his eyes and stumbles at Shea's feet.

"Harold! It's all over," moans the breathless Czech. "Those—things—just ate Snag, and the sailors are almost all gone!" Shea looks to the top of the hill before them. Sycorax stands there smiling, holding her crooked staff defiantly in the air.

Turn to section 77.

* 5 *

Shea pauses to think. The witch was dead before Prospero came to the island in Shakespeare's play. Why shouldn't Harold Shea be the messenger of her destruction? On the other hand, she was asleep with her baby at her side. . . .

"Harold, if you cannot, I shall do the deed!" Belphebe whispers resolutely. Shea steels his nerve and grabs the axe from her hands. He tiptoes over to the witch's bed and lifts the heavy blade into the air. He pauses again.

Sycorax's eyes flash open and stare ominously into his. Shea is paralyzed. The witch begins to scream in a high-pitched, shrill voice. Harold comes to life and drops the axe, motions to Belphebe, and runs for the door.

Turn to section 69.

Section 6

* 6 *

The occasional torch set into the wall in this section of the cave illuminates a variety of lifelike statuary; some look freshly carved, some are headless and limbless. A small stream trickles noisily down the center of the path. Belphebe stops Shea with an outstretched hand. Just to the right of them, barely visible, is a side tunnel. The floor of the passage is heavily scored with footprints leading into the tunnel.

If Harold and Belphebe ignore the side passage, turn to section 54.

If they explore the side passage, turn to section 20.

* 7 *

Shea circles around the bush twice, with the harpy right behind him. Finally, the harpy wises up and flies over the top of the bush, landing in front of him. Shea turns and runs back the way he came. He bounds over a log and almost clears another, but his foot catches on a branch and he tumbles to the ground. The creature is directly above him now, hissing malevolently. Twigs and dirt cloud the air, stirred up by the great wings.

Shea crawls to his knees; escape seems hopeless. And then, before him, almost in his hands, lies a large dead branch . . . the club he threw away! In a flash, he grabs it and stands up to face the monster.

Turn to section 33.

* 8 *

Belphebe shudders and puts her arms around him. Large black clouds boil overhead, conjured out of nowhere. The air becomes still and damp, and the goblins fall silent. The crackling forest fire is all that can be heard. Even the witch Sycorax looks warily into the sky. A blinding flash of lightning strikes, followed immediately by a deafening clap of thunder.

A fine mist fills the air, and that soon turns to rain, which quickly becomes an unbelievable downpour. It is almost as though they are standing under Niagara Falls. Shea grabs Belphebe's hand. He can hardly even see her. The ground on which they are standing becomes a river, and rushing water swirls around their legs. The spirits put their arms around Shea and Belphebe and pull them along to higher ground just as a wall of water, laden with logs and broken trees, washes across the valley.

Later, after the rain has stopped and the flash flood has subsided, a sodden Shea surveys the desolation below. The forest fire is out all right, and the goblins have been washed away. But so has half the country-

Section 8

side, and the grassy field has turned into a litter-strewn, muddy swamp. Bitter-Root and Quamoclit are wringing out Belphebe's clothes.

"I think I got the decimal point wrong on that one," Shea says humbly.

"Ist the fire not drowned, and our enemies gone with the flood!" says Quamoclit.

"Yes, Harold," chimes Belphebe, "the day is ours!"

Shea keeps thinking of another line from Shakespeare: "The quality of mercy is not strain'd. . . ." Today it did more than droppeth gently from heaven upon the place beneath!

Turn to section 64.

Section 9

* 9 *

The largest of the three ugly creatures rushes at Shea, bellowing what must be a goblin war cry. Belphebe deftly sweeps the torch in front of its face and it trips and falls into the pile of skulls. The two remaining goblins run at Shea, who sidesteps the first and clobbers the second on the head with a resounding thump.

After a little fancy footwork, Shea catches the second goblin with its guard down. With a lunge that would have been better suited to a pointed weapon, Shea rams the end of his club into the goblin's gut. It falls to the floor, clutching its stomach and screaming loudly.

The goblin that has fallen into the pile of skulls is struggling to its feet. Shea maneuvers around behind it and delivers a blow that sends the goblin to the ground for keeps.

"Nice work, champion!" says Belphebe with a smile. Shea sits down on a rock to catch his breath.

"I hope we didn't wake any more of these suckers," he puffs. Belphebe is walking around the room, poking at the goblin bedding with her foot. She bends down suddenly and grabs something.

Section 9

"A fine prize for your victory, Harold." She returns holding a rusty Italian rapier. Shea grabs it and dances across the floor, flourishing the weapon.

"Not bad balance," he says with a grin. "It's almost as good as my épée. Thanks a lot, Toots!"

Belphebe leads them out the far end of the room and down a narrow tunnel. It winds down and to the left, then empties out into a much larger section of cavern.

"Methinks down is the way to travel," whispers Belphebe. Shea agrees.

Add a +1 sword (the rapier) to the list of Harold's possessions.

Turn to section 54.

Section 10

* 10 *

Shea is not about to follow a disgruntled goblin into the depths of a volcano.

"Sorry, pal," says Shea. "My path lies yonder," and he sprints off for the entrance, preferring daylight to darkness. Along the way, he is joined by two of his own simulacrons who obviously share the same thought. Moments later, he and himselves dash out into the blinding daylight and run headlong into the two guards at the door.

TWO GOBLINS
To hit Shea: 14   To be hit: 11   Hit points: 3 each

Damage with clubs: D6

Shea fights with his bare hands and does D6−1 damage if he hits.

Shea's simulacrons fight alongside him (giving him three rolls to hit) for the first two rounds, then they disappear. For these first two rounds, roll D6 each time a goblin scores a hit. On a roll of a 1 or 2, the goblin hits the real Shea. Any other result is a hit on a simulacron. You don't need to keep a record of their hits.

Section 10

If all the goblin guards are not dead at the end of a round, they are joined in the next round by one more (fresh) guard.

If Harold decides to jump down the side of the hill and take his chances on the fall, turn to section 23.

If Harold wins the fight, turn to section 36.

If Harold is killed, turn to section 29.

Section 11

* 11 *

"Hang on a minute, ladies," Shea says. "I don't intend to stumble around in the dark holding onto a unicorn's tail!" He steps over to the stream. Using wet sand, he quickly fashions a crude model of a horse's head, leaving out the stick for a horn that had brought him a rhino the last time. Shea crouches over his handiwork, gesturing as he recites:

> "Oh, steed that feeds on reeds,
>   And drinks the whirlpool's surge,
> In the name of the horse of Ceres,
>   I conjure you now, emerge!"

He pauses a moment, immersed in deep thought, and then continues:

> "Strong, yet of me subservient,
>   Bring a horse without a horn,
> Up from this small river,
>   I conjure you . . . be born!"

The model and the stream nearby burst into a cloud of spray and sand. Harold figures the horse of Ceres would be some sort

Section 11

of plowhorse. As the spray falls to the ground, a deep grunt reveals that his magic has succeeded . . . to a certain degree.

Staring at him blankly from the stream is a full-grown hippopotamus!

Belphebe bursts into laughter. Shea winces. There is no turning back now. So he's summoned a hippo. Well, he'll ride a hippo! Besides, it is supposed to be subservient. Shea steps back and leaps onto the hippo's back. The enormous creature lets out a basso profundo yell and begins waddling rapidly downstream.

Shea bounces around spread-eagled on the broad back and hangs on for dear life, the memory of his ride on the bull rhino flashing before his eyes. There must be some way to control this thing.

Roll 3 D6 and compare the result to Harold's Strength value.

If the total of the dice is the same as or lower than Harold's Strength, turn to section 48.

If the total is greater, turn to section 82.

Section 12

* **12** *

Shea lands with a crash in the thorny scrub. It is thicker than it looks from above, and he plows through several layers of thornbush. At last his feet hit the ground, and he has to struggle to extricate himself from the tangled mass of vegetation. Once free, he takes off running down the valley. Perspiration stings the tiny cuts the thorns have made on his hands and cheeks.

Shea splashes into a brackish creek and turns upstream, hoping to cover his footprints. He soon slows to a walk as the light and his energy give out. He can no longer hear any pursuers. With his last bit of strength, Shea struggles up the bank and into a grassy clearing, where he curls up into a ball in some tall weeds and falls promptly asleep.

The first rays of a sunny morning climb over a hill and shine cheerfully down on Shea. He opens his eyes with a start, then shivers and remembers where he is. He has been dreaming of an automobile chase. Belphebe is driving their Chevrolet, and he is in the back seat while she takes corners on

Section 12

two wheels . . . Belphebe! He has to find her. Shea sits up, rubbing his hands together to generate some heat. His empty stomach complains, and he crawls over to the creek for a drink. There are brown things floating in the water. He doesn't know what they are and doesn't care; the water tastes good.

Shea stretches his sore muscles and washes his scratches before setting out upstream again. Now that the sun is out, he can tell that he was traveling north the night before. He travels in the valley by the creek for over an hour, occasionally climbing a hill to survey his position. There are no goblins to be seen, but neither can he spot the green trees of the land of the spirits.

It is nearly noon when Shea climbs a particularly high brush-covered hill. What he sees makes him drop quietly to the ground. Not fifty yards away are some old ruins consisting of columns, a couple of crumbling buildings, and a large, flat tiled floor upon which some goblins are playing what looks like a game of shuffleboard.

Shea watches with interest for a while. Then the smell of cooked food attacks his nose, and he begins working his way closer by ducking from one bush to the next. Soon, he can make out their conversation. He slips behind a crumbling building. Inside, the goblin meal is cooking in a pot over a small fire.

Section 12

Shea is on the verge of sneaking in to steal some food when a fight breaks out on the shuffleboard court. One of the goblins has been caught cheating, and the others jump on the villain. The hapless goblin is tied upside down to a column, where it retches and moans while the game continues. Shea actually begins to feel sorry for the creature. A wild idea comes to mind.

Shea stands up, arranges his suit as best he can, and walks boldly out onto the forum. The two goblins spot him immediately, and one drops his stick in amazement.

"Good morning, boys," Shea begins. "I've been watching your game. You're both pretty talented players. I, myself, was once the All-Ohio shuffleboard champion." He bends over and picks up the dropped stick. "You see, in Ohio, this game is also known as the national pastime." Shea leans forward and shoves a rock skillfully across the court. "My name ranks right up there with the all-time greats such as Lou Gehrig, Babe Ruth, and Joe DiMaggio. . . ."

"Loo Gerik?" asks the smaller goblin, its eyes wide open.

The other comes to its senses. "Ho, you be the mage sought by the witch. 'Tis a trick." It nudges its smaller companion.

"I'll make you a wager," Shea goes on. "I'll take on the better of you. If I win, you cut down your noisy companion over there."

Section 12

He points at the goblin hanging from the column. "Then you give me a meal, and I'm gone."

"And if I win . . ." says the larger goblin defiantly.

"I'm your prisoner."

The game begins, and it soon becomes clear that Shea is up against a master. Each time they shoot, Harold's stones are consistently knocked off the mark by those of the goblin. Shea considers using magic to assist his cause.

Roll 3 D6 and compare the result to Harold's Wisdom value.

If the total of the dice is the same as or lower than Harold's Wisdom, turn to section 35.

If the total of the dice is greater, turn to section 19.

Section 13

* 13 *

Belphebe crushes Harold in her arms. "Oh, dearest, I thought you would be killed," she says breathlessly. "Yet our plight has only grown worse since you arrived. Can you not think of some powerful spell to save us, Harold?"

A goblin spear fells a sailor who stands mere paces away. Shea's mind is a blur. There must be something he can do.... The Dolan Doom spell?

"Can you not summon beasts to our aid?" asks Belphebe as she fires an arrow at the enemy. Shea makes up his mind.

If Harold tries to summon a herd of rhinos, turn to section 4.

If Harold tries to cast the Dolan Doom spell (last used in the land of Faerie) turn to section 77.

* 14 *

The dead zone created by the witch has a queer, depressing effect on Shea. As he winds his way up, down, and around the hilly terrain, not a single living tree can be seen. The only plants are the various brown and olive drab thornbushes, and even these seem only half alive. The overcast sky only adds to the general gloom.

The day wears on, and Shea stops for a drink from a murky stream. His empty stomach growls, but he has seen no edible plants, and the rats and lizards he encounters manage to escape his clumsy attempts at capture. But at least he hasn't met any goblins or other servants of Sycorax.

Just as he is thinking about how alone he is, Shea reaches the top of a high hill and sees a long line of creatures, probably goblins, streaming back and forth along the trail to the northwest. Beyond the busy trail rise taller hills, mostly covered with diseased and burned timber.

To the northeast are the lush green forests of the spirits. Even as he gazes on the beautiful forest, the sun breaks through the clouds and shines cheerfully on the living half of

Section 14

the island. Shea sits down to catch his breath.

If Harold heads northwest toward Sycorax's cave, turn to section 57.

If Harold heads northeast toward the spirit cave, turn to section 3.

* 15 *

"Psst! Hey you!" Shea calls out to a sullen-looking goblin who has been watching the attempts to make a fire. It ambles toward Shea with a puzzled look on its face. "Yeah, you! I can show you how to make a fire. You'll be a big shot."

The goblin kneels down next to Shea. "What wouldst thou, prisoner?" growls the goblin. "'Tis too damp for fire."

"Maybe for you guys. But I know some magic tricks that'll get you a roaring blaze in no time."

"So show me," the goblin answers.

"Ya gotta untie me first, so I can work the spells . . . and don't worry, I won't run away, either," says Shea.

"You take me for a fool," snickers the goblin, and it gives Shea a swift kick in the ribs as it walks back to the group. Shea's lighter falls out into the grass.

Later, a bowl of muddy water is poured in the general direction of Shea's mouth, and that is his supper. He spends an incredibly miserable night with his hands and feet still bound to the pole.

Section 15

Remove the lighter from Harold's list of possessions.

Turn to section 47.

* 16 *

Shea is aware that they entered the mouth of a limestone cavern. More phosphorescent fairies appear, casting a dim but pleasant glow in the rock chamber.

"I'll bet this saves on your electric bill," says Shea as they set out again by fairy-light. Bitter-Root leads them on, escorted by her amber friends. Fairies of several shades of green float around Belphebe, while Shea's path is lit by a solitary red globe.

"We spirits are not by choice dwellers of the earth," says Bitter-Root. She has turned to face Harold and Belphebe and is flying effortlessly backward into the cave. "'Tis said Setebos himself liv'd here in times bygone. Yet now we come and are safe from the witch's fury."

The spirit flies up to a ledge above them and tosses down a rope ladder. "I fear you must climb where I may soar." Shea wonders who needs a rope ladder when all the inhabitants seem to be able to fly. Climbing up the ladder behind his wife, he notices sadly what the short time in this world has done to Belphebe's expensive dress. She has

Section 16

tied what remains of it together around her legs.

They walk along a narrow ledge and then turn into a smaller tunnel. This new passage slopes down to join two side tunnels which branch in from above. Bitter-Root continues on and soon they are in an enormous room illuminated by hundreds of glowing fairies. The roof is covered by stalactites which merge with stalagmites around the edges to form thick, multicolored columns that shimmer in the fairy glow.

As Shea looks about him, he notices Polacek on the far side of the room, seated at a thick wooden table across from a swarthy dark-haired man. They are playing a game of chess. Vaclav spots the new arrivals. "Hiya, Harold, Belphebe! Welcome to fairyland." The dark man twists his thick black beard between his fingers, studying the chessboard intently. "This is Snag, a sailor from Naples," Polacek continues. "You'll have to forgive him. We're playing timed moves, and we've got a hot bet going."

Sitting crosslegged on the table, watching the game, is a male spirit. He motions to Shea and Belphebe. "Come, be seated and partake of our wine!" Bitter-Root has already drifted over to the table and is filling two goblets. "My name is Moonwort." The male spirit effortlessly flies up from the table and lands in front of Belphebe. "I am blest in

Section 16

your acquaintance." He turns to Shea. "Master Pollychek has told me how you come from so far to our aid."

As they sit down, Snag makes an unintelligible noise, moves a piece, and turns a small hourglass sideways on the table. "Your go, Polish." The sailor grabs Shea's hand and shakes it heartily. "All hail, great master. Your reputation doth precede you. Now will we make short work of that miserable Sycorax!" The sailor has paws the size of baseball mitts.

Bitter-Root passes out the wine and speaks: "Here before thee is the only man we have saved from the witch. As his ship split upon the rocks, Moonwort and I carried him off unseen. His companions are all now stones by the beach."

The wine is light and sweet. Polacek is frowning at the game. Shea observes that the Czech is several pieces down, and Snag has accumulated a pile of American coins.

"Marry, Bitter-Root, is this all you number?" Belphebe asks with concern.

The she-spirit nods sadly. "Aye, good Quamoclit stands watch on the hill. With her, we are but three, and the sailor." A blue fairy dances in front of them. "Yea, and the fairies . . . and now, thou. Pray what shall we do?" The spirit looks into Shea's eyes.

The wine dances in his empty stomach and makes him lightheaded. "How about

Section 16

breakfast, for starters," answers Shea. "Then we can make our plans." Snag looks up from the game and nods in agreement.

The two spirits vanish immediately. Moments later they reappear, each holding a large silver tray laden with food, which they set before their guests. Harold and Belphebe help themselves to bread and cheese and joints of meat, while the chess game continues. Two more moves, however, and Vaclav is forced to surrender after losing his queen and another fifty cents. Snag stuffs his winnings into a leather pouch and proceeds to devour an entire roast bird.

Shea leans back and speaks: "As I see it, we need to figure out a way to get that book back from Sycorax. We can practice our magic without it"—he shoots Vaclav a dirty glance—"but I don't want that witch to have access to the accumulated magical knowledge of six other worlds."

Polacek grimaces. "It may be too late already, Harold. You can read those symbols in any language."

The meal continues in a somewhat more somber mood. Looking about, Shea notices the spirits are not eating and wonders if conjured meals have any actual substance to them. The food feels real enough inside him, and Snag finishes his meal with several deep, satisfied belches.

After questioning Bitter-Root and Moon-

Section 16

wort to some length, Shea learns that Sycorax summons a storm every fortnight to blow sailors and their ships to doom. The effort, however, drains the witch so completely that she spends the next day sleeping in her cave to regain her power. That, it seems, would be the best time to slip in and regain the precious magic book.

It is soon ascertained that they have two days before Sycorax brews up her next batch of meteorological mischief.

That afternoon finds the four humans out in the woods preparing aircraft. Flying broomsticks are a specialty of Shea's and, for once, he has time to build them slowly and carefully. High-speed two-seaters are what he has in mind.

Snag and Polacek tramp into the forest and return with two straight, young oak saplings. With some diligent pruning, these are turned into very large broomsticks. Bundles of straw gathered by Quamoclit are tied to the ends. Belphebe and Bitter-Root contribute eagle feathers, which are securely fastened fore and aft. Finally, short crosspieces are attached using strong vines.

"Votsy, you and Snag watch," says Shea. "Belphebe and I will take one up and show you how it's done." Polacek is noticeably unhappy, but his humbling experience as a purple cow is fresh in his memory and he is content to let Harold run the show.

Section 16

The three spirits hover overhead as Shea straddles his broom, makes mystic passes, and begins to recite:

"Bird of the Aerie, ruler of skye;
  Lend us your wings, so we too may fly."

The broom jerks in his hands and begins to vibrate. Shea looks behind him. Belphebe is astride her end, holding on for dear life.

He looks across to Polacek. "That's just what you say to get the engine warmed up, Votsy," states Harold. "This next part gets you airborne. Once you're up, use your body to steer." Shea makes more passes and chants:

"By oak, ash, and maple,
  The high air through,
 Show me you're able
  To fly swiftly and true!"

The broom responds quickly and angles skyward with a rush. Belphebe yelps. Shea leans to the left and his broom circles tightly around the hovering spirits. He pulls back and the broom goes into a tight loop.

"Harold!" cries an anguished Belphebe as he levels off at treetop height. Shea is pleased. This broom is faster and handles better than any he has made before. The double set of eagle feathers probably ac-

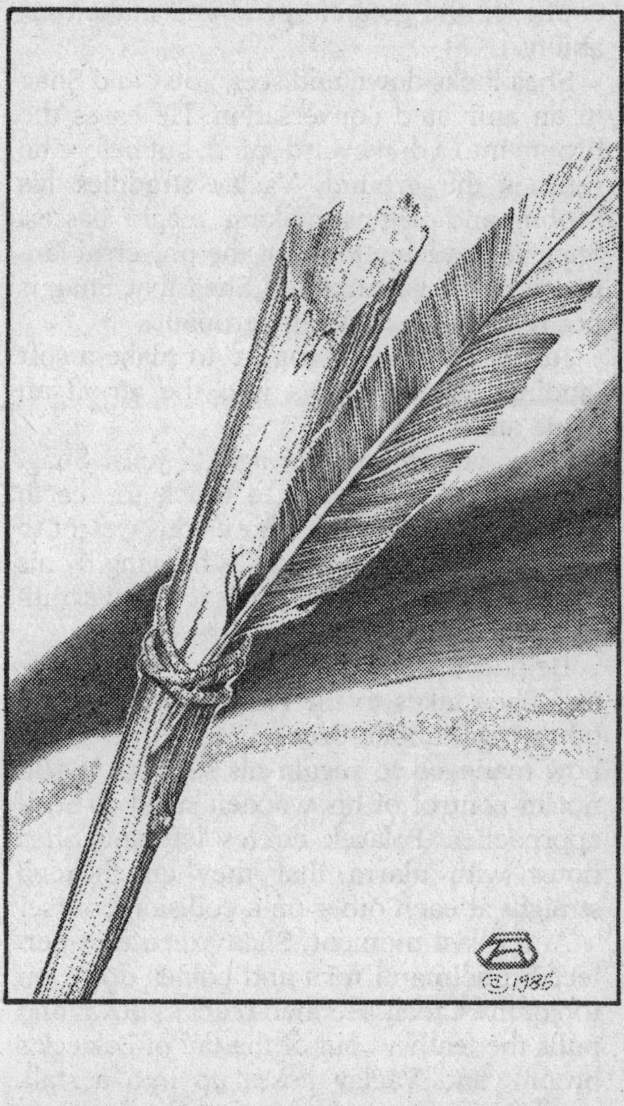

Section 16

count for the greater speed and maneuverability.

Shea looks down and sees Votsy and Snag in an animated conversation. He eases the broom into a downward spiral, but before he reaches the ground, Vaclav straddles his broom and begins making magic passes. Snag is gesturing too, but the universal language of his gestures tell Shea that Snag is not ready to become an aeronaut.

Just as Shea is nosing up to make a soft landing, Vaclav shoots into the air at an acute angle.

"We have another wager," yells Snag. "That he shall not live to touch the earth again!" A scream from above adds weight to Snag's conviction. Polacek is hanging by his fingers beneath the broom as it plows erratically up and down through the treetops.

Belphebe hops off as soon as she is able and Shea takes to the air in pursuit of the bouncing Rubber Czech. Vaclav has somehow managed to regain his seat but is still not in control of his wooden steed as Shea approaches. Polacek circles left and Shea notes with alarm that they are headed straight at each other on a collision course!

At the last moment, Shea executes a perfect Immelmann turn and comes down on top of the Czech. He then reaches down and pulls the feathers out of the tail of Polacek's broom, and Vaclav noses up into a stall.

Section 16

While Shea circles effortlessly back to the ground, the Czech comes spinning down into a clump of juniper bushes.

It takes most of the evening to persuade Snag to ride with Polacek. But on his third flight, Votsy performs some complex aerobatics without incident, and even Shea is convinced that the Czech has finally learned to fly the broom.

That night, after another fine spirit-summoned supper, Shea learns that the spirits will not accompany them on their journey to the witch's side of the island. They dare not venture near Sycorax for fear of being put under a spell as happened to Ariel.

They awaken before dawn and assemble at the mouth of the cave. There is ample evidence of the witch's antics. The trees are lashed by wild winds and rain falls in heavy torrents.

"Can we fly in this weather?" Belphebe asks with concern.

Harold looks up at the sky. "We'll soon find out!"

Bitter-Root flutters up and hands Shea a lock of her hair tied with a golden thread. "Take thee this," says the spirit, "and if thou see'st Ariel, show't. Perchance he will return to us."

Shea stuffs the lock into his breast pocket. Vaclav and Snag walk their broom out into the rain, which has eased up considerably.

Section 16

They straddle it and wave at Shea.

"I'm ready," Belphebe says from behind. Moments later, the two brooms and their passengers spiral skyward, with the spirits and several colorful fairies flying in company. They rise above the hills until Shea can see great waves covered with whitecaps in the sea around the island.

The rain and wind make the flight uncomfortable, but the brooms handle well. As they fly west, the green forests give way to an endless vista of dead and dying trees. The division between the lands of Sycorax and that of the spirits is very clear indeed.

Shea looks to either side and notices the fairies are gone. Vaclav and Snag zoom across in front of him. The Czech says something and gestures earthward. Shea can't understand a word, but follows Vaclav as he spirals down. It is raining harder now. The two brooms cruise above the dead treetops and then circle to a landing atop the crown of a high hill.

The wind howls, and large drops of rain drench them as the four seek cover behind a rock outcrop.

"I saw the witch!" yells Polacek as he crouches next to Snag. Shea can just barely hear him through the noise of the storm. "She's over there on the next hill!" Vaclav says, pointing at the rock behind which they are hiding.

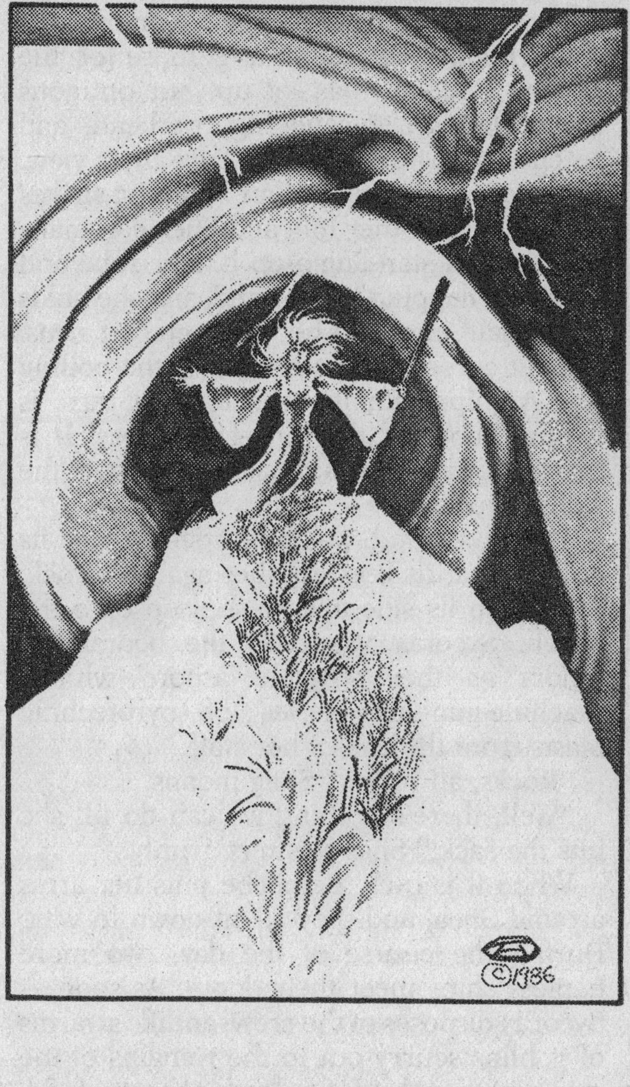
©1986

Section 16

As one, they all stand up and lean over the rock, hoping to catch a glimpse of the enemy. The rain has let up, but ominous black clouds are scudding overhead, and patches of fog and mist obscure their view. Just then, a frightful bolt of lightning strikes the top of the other hill, and Shea can make out Sycorax standing atop it. Her robe and cloak are flapping in the wind, and she holds a long staff in one of her outstretched arms.

Snag curses and points out at the boiling sea. A ship, with its sails torn to rags, is tossing about in the forty-foot waves. It is being blown inexorably ashore toward the waiting rocks.

They wait and watch the ship meet its doom. After its keel smashes against a rock, it rolls on its side and washes up onto the beach. Sycorax vaporizes the bedraggled sailors as they struggle ashore with a machine-gun–like series of pyrotechnic blasts from the end of her staff.

"Rocks, all rocks." Snag moans.

"Well, there's nothing we can do till she hits the sack!" Shea answers grimly.

When it is over, Belphebe puts her arms around Shea, and they all sit down to wait. During the course of the day, two more hapless ships meet their doom. As soon as Sycorax disposes of the crew, antlike swarms of goblins scurry out to the remains of the ship and carry back armloads of cargo, food,

Section 16

and miscellaneous loot. The long lines of goblins disappear into the roots of the hill upon which Sycorax stands. Shea hopes he can find an entrance that isn't quite so busy.

It is drizzling as they open the lunch that Bitter-Root has prepared for them. Belphebe stands watch over the hill, while Snag and Polacek make pigs of themselves. When Shea rises to give Belphebe an apple, she points anxiously.

"Shhh!" she whispers. "Two goblins approach."

Coming through the thornbushes are two ugly dark green creatures with heavy clubs resting on their shoulders. They are hotly engaged in discussion, and one seems ready to use his club on his companion.

Snag appears at Shea's side. "Let's take them!" he says, with blood in his eyes.

If they try to avoid the goblin guards, turn to section 72.

If they try to overwhelm the guards, turn to section 2.

Section 17

* 17 *

Shea follows his nose and walks on through the center passage, which descends in a series of winding curves. He feels like he is walking down a hole made by a drunken worm. The ever-freshening air makes him glad he chose this path.

A narrow side passage presents itself on the right.

If Shea takes the side path, turn to section 75.

If Shea continues on the main path, turn to section 32.

* 18 *

"Pentacles near and pentacles far,
  Now disappear from where you are!
Shemhamporesh!"

The door creaks inward slightly. Just then, however, the sound of bare feet slapping against clay comes from all directions. Shea turns to see several yellow-eyed goblins coming toward them out of the darkness.

FOUR GOBLINS
To hit Shea: 14   To be hit: 11   Hit points: 3 each

Damage with clubs: D6 (If Shea has no sword, he also does D6 damage when he hits.)

Belphebe keeps one or two of the goblins busy until there is only one left. Two goblins attack Shea each round until two are slain.

Belphebe inflicts one point of damage to any one goblin she engages during a round (your choice).

If Harold wins using a +1 sword, turn to section 38.

Section 18

If Harold wins without having a sword, turn to section 30.

If Harold is killed, turn to section 29.

* 19 *

Harold recalls, from one of his earlier adventures, the way Heimdall had used magic to cheat in the cockroach races back in Surt's stronghold. Shea is fairly certain he can do likewise at shuffleboard. He mumbles discreetly and makes passes with his left hand. The large goblin's rocks consistently slide past the mark, while Shea's stones stop with mysterious regularity on the highest score. When his total score becomes larger than that of the goblin, it throws its stick to the deck in anger.

"Damnation! You cozen me, and would dance out of your true debt," the goblin snarls. "Gretio, this sheep-biter needeth thrashing!" It motions to the smaller goblin.

TWO GOBLINS
To hit Shea: 14   To be hit: 11   Hit points: 3 each

Damage with fists: D6−1

After each round of this fight, Harold may try to escape. Roll 3 D6. If the total of the dice is the same as or lower than Harold's Dexterity value, turn to section 58.

Section 19

If the total of the dice is higher than Harold's Dexterity, the fight continues.

If Harold wins the fight, turn to section 53.

If Harold dies, turn to section 29.

* 20 *

The tiny side passage leads steeply upward for nearly fifty feet, then turns left and opens into a room. As Belphebe moves her torch, the light reveals stacks of wooden barrels, chests, and other booty taken from the ships. The glint of metal catches Shea's eye.

"Over there," he says excitedly. The two of them rush to a corner of the room. There on the floor is a pile of swords and other edged weapons. Shea pulls a slender rapier out of the pile.

He smiles as he waves it about, making passes at an invisible enemy. "Almost as good as my épée! Those Italians know how to make fine weapons."

Belphebe shushes him, but takes a small jeweled dagger for herself. "Let's be on with our quest, Harold," she reminds him. A brief search reveals that the only way out is the way they came. As they descend the path, Belphebe stops Shea again.

"Voices," she whispers. They stand motionless for a long moment. Then Belphebe relaxes, saying, "They have passed." Shea leans over and kisses her cheek. Her keen hearing comes in handy at times like this.

Section 20

They walk slowly out into the main passageway.

Add a +1 sword (the rapier) to the list of Harold's possessions.

Turn to section 54.

* 21 *

Sometime later that night, Shea awakes to the sound of voices. The fire is burning low and he can dimly see Belphebe, but no one else. Vaclav? He sits up abruptly.

"Hello?"

Belphebe answers, "Good morrow, Harold. We are joined by a friend." Directly across from her he can just make out a wispy, female form. It is wearing next to nothing, has golden hair . . . and enormous, shimmering wings. He leans forward and squints for a better view.

"Greetings, good sir," says the creature in a soft voice. "I am called Bitter-Root. Welcome to our island." She extends her hand. Shea reaches out and touches her gently.

"Harold Shea, at your service." He smiles. "I guess you and Belphebe are acquainted. So where are we? Is this Prospero's island?"

"I know not of Prospero. This be the isle of Setebos; a happy place, once, liv'd in by sprites and spirits and the beasts in peace and harmony. But now we are set upon by the wretched Sycorax, who doth bespoil the trees and the land with pricking-goss and brine pits. . . ."

©1986

Section 21

"Wait a minute!" Shea interrupts. "You mean to say that witch is still alive and kicking?"

"Would that she were perish'd. The vile hag hath raised legions of foul goblins and taken our fair Ariel to her dirty service. I fear 'twas Ariel, himself, who stole your book for her. But Belphebe has spoken much of your brave deeds. Surely such a great mage as thyself needs not his library."

"I wouldn't be too sure of that," Shea says with a wry grin. "So far our magic hasn't been too successful here." He pauses a moment and rubs his chin. "So there's a war between you guys and Sycorax?"

The spirit looks confused. "I know not of war. That Sycorax is evil there is no doubt. Her storms on the seas bring shipwreck'd sailors. These she turns to stones and plants. Those spirits who refuse her chores are lock'd in the hearts of trees to suffer and cry."

Shea looks around into the woods. "Are we safe here, Bitter-Root?"

"Aye, fortune brought you to our side of the island. Her magic is not so strong in these woods. The unicorns hold back the goblins. But now that Ariel's her servant, I fear all's lost."

Shea thinks about Vaclav. "I don't suppose you've seen a large purple cow wandering around anywhere?"

Section 21

Belphebe laughs. "'Twas he who sent Bitter-Root unto us."

"Certes," says the spirit. "We found him near our cell. 'Twas but a simple task to make him right."

Shea mumbles something obscene under his breath. He can just picture the Czech laying on his back while a bevy of beautiful, half-naked spirits stuff peeled grapes into his mouth.

Bitter-Root suggests they follow her to her cell, a cave which was not too far away. A unicorn is called to carry Belphebe.

"What about me?" asks Shea. "Don't I get a lift?" When the spirit begins to explain the unicorns' intense dislike of men, Shea interrupts. "Yeah, yeah, I know all that," says Shea.

Belphebe pats her mount and smiles at her husband. "Here's a guide you may hold," she says, indicating the unicorn's tail. "Or would'st conjure yourself a ry . . . ryenocery as you did in Loselwood?"

He winces, recalling the rhino he accidentally summoned for a mount in Faerie. Quite handy at the time, but the situation didn't really call for a Sherman tank. Maybe if he changed the spell a little bit.

If Shea tries to summon a mount, turn to section 11.

Section 21

If Shea tries to avoid the possibility of an embarrassing spell failure and follows Belphebe, holding the unicorn's tail, turn to section 28.

Section 22

* **22** *

Trusting the advice of Malovio, although he isn't sure why, Shea follows the left path, which leads up and winds around as it climbs. The upward trek seems never-ending, and Shea stops to catch his breath. Has the goblin sent him off in the wrong direction? He decides to press on for a while longer. Soon, he comes to a large room. At last!

Holding up his torch, Harold can make out the shadowy bulk of the sleeping fire drake. Ever so cautiously, he steps forward into the room.

Roll 3 D6 and compare the result to Harold's Intelligence value.

If the total of the dice is the same as or lower than Harold's Intelligence, turn to section 37.

If the total is greater, turn to section 67.

* 23 *

Shea throws caution to the winds. Ducking under the swinging club of the nearest goblin, he leaps, feet first, over the side of the mountain and plummets down the cinder slope. He slides rapidly, and he likens the experience to sliding down a ski slope after falling off his skis. At last he bounces over a rock and falls several feet before crashing into a pile of gravel.

Roll 1 D6. The number rolled is the number of hit points of damage Harold sustains in the fall. Subtract this number from the total on Shea's record sheet.

If Harold survives the fall, turn to section 79.

If Harold is killed by the fall, turn to section 29.

* 24 *

Belphebe shudders and puts her arms around him. Large black clouds boil overhead, conjured out of nowhere. The air becomes still and damp, and the goblins fall silent. The crackling forest fire is all that can be heard. Even the witch Sycorax looks warily into the sky. A blinding flash of lightning strikes, followed immediately by a deafening clap of thunder. Tiny black particles begin falling from the cloud. They increase in size, and large blobs of soot descend from the heavens. Soon everything is covered by a fine blanket of black.

The sooty fallout seems to have no effect on the fire, and the goblins break out in raucous cheers. Shea shakes his head in disgust just as a rock tossed by one of the goblins conks him on the head.

Subtract one hit point from Harold's total on the record sheet.

If Harold survives, turn to section 40.

If Harold dies, turn to section 29.

* 25 *

More cautiously than ever, Shea follows Belphebe's carefully chosen footsteps. She adroitly sidesteps a pile of human skulls. Unfortunately, Harold manages to clip the bottom of the pile with his toe. The skulls rattle noisily as they tumble across the floor.

"Harold!" hisses Belphebe angrily. The goblins are stirring. One of them cries out. Shea spies a goblin club near the skulls and picks it up. He and Belphebe back away slowly as three goblins come out of the darkness.

THREE GOBLINS
To hit Shea: 14   To be hit: 11   Hit points: 3 each

Damage with clubs: D6

Belphebe keeps one of the goblins at bay with her torch until there is only one goblin left. Until one goblin is slain, two attack Shea each round.

If Harold wins the fight, turn to section 9.

If Harold is killed, turn to section 29.

Section 26

* 26 *

"Psst! Hey you!" Shea calls out to a sullen-looking goblin who has been watching the attempts to make a fire. It ambles toward Shea with a puzzled look on its face. "Yeah, you! I can show you how to make a fire. You'll be a big shot."

The goblin kneels down next to Shea. "What wouldst thou, prisoner?" growls the goblin. "'Tis too damp for fire."

"Maybe for you guys. But I know some magic tricks that'll get you a roaring blaze in no time."

"So show me," the goblin answers.

"Ya gotta untie me first, so I can work the spells . . . and don't worry, I won't run away, either," says Shea persuasively.

A little more haggling follows before Shea sighs with relief as his hands are untied. He gives his lighter to the goblin and shows the creature how it works. It is enormously pleased and stands up to rush over and show its companions.

Shea grabs it by the arm and says, "Hey, wait, that's only half the show. Now we gotta make some fire-water to go with that. I need a bucket of water and some wood." Shea

Section 26

unties his feet while the goblin goes off for the water.

It returns with a dented pewter bowl, half full of muddy water. Shea places it ceremoniously on the ground and drops in some broken bits of tree branch. On a larger piece, he scratches out some letters with a rock:

$$H\,H\,H\,H$$
$$H\,C\,C\,C\,C\,H$$
$$H\,H\,H\,H$$

He thinks a while longer. It has been some time since he'd taken organic chemistry. The stuff he wants is made of several complex molecules. He scratches out the formulas for an isoparaffin, a naphthene, and an olefin. Shea begins stirring the mixture with the large stick and recites:

"As from the ground comes the bubbling well,
The nectar of Standard and Phillips and Shell,
Internal combustion, petroleum's jewel.
Change now, I command thee, to high-octane fuel!"

The color of the liquid suddenly darkens, and some of the goblins who are watching murmur in awe. Shea sniffs his concoction.

Section 26

It smells potent enough. He hands the bowl to the goblin with the lighter.

"Place this on top of your pile of wood over there and do your stuff." He wiggles his thumb at the goblin and winks. The goblins all walk off, and Shea begins to edge away, waiting for the fateful click.

Remove the lighter from Harold's list of possessions.

The resulting pillar of fire causes quite a stir. Flaming goblins run about screaming. Shea slips quietly off into the bushes and then scoots up and over a gravel-covered hill, ripping his pants on a thornbush as he runs. He can hear goblins following him.

There are fewer thornbushes along the top of the hill and Shea makes better progress. Goblins are running below him now, cursing his very existence. The slope curves sharply upward. Shea finds himself rock-climbing, and his pursuers are halfway up the hill.

Shea stops and his heart sinks. Before him is a thirty-foot drop, and at the bottom are masses of thick brambles. A rock whizzes past his head. He swallows the lump in his throat and leaps over the edge.

Roll 3 D6 and compare the result to Harold's Constitution value.

Section 26

If the total of the dice is the same as or lower than Harold's Constitution value, turn to section 12.

If the total of the dice is higher, turn to section 85.

* 27 *

Harold Shea dreams he is packed in a snowbank. It is deep and cold, and he is frozen solid. He can see little snowmen with coal eyes and carrot noses building an igloo around him. . . .

He wakes to find himself buried up to the neck in a low mound of dirt near the bank of the stream. The back of his head throbs as though it has been used as the ball in the Army/Navy football game. He shivers and tries to move. Nothing. He is trapped. It is almost as if the earth has opened up and swallowed him. There is grass around him, and the soil is not broken.

He cranes his head painfully from side to side. No sign of Vaclav or Belphebe. He can see the rock he is sitting on. There is his club, but the book of magic seems to be gone.

He yells for Belphebe and then listens carefully. No answer. After calling a while longer, his head begins to pound so horribly that he has to stop. How does one get oneself out of the cold ground, he wonders. He remembers being buried in the sand up at Headlands Beach by Lake Erie in happier

Section 27

times. Then, he wriggled himself free, but he wasn't so deeply buried. He begins moving his neck in a circular motion, pushing back a small amount of dirt. At that rate, he will be there a long time.

A stick snaps in the woods nearby. He freezes. Out of the forest lopes a medium-sized gray wolf. It sniffs around in the grass for a moment and then heads straight for Shea.

So this is it. The great Harold Shea is about to meet his end, chewed up by a wolf while buried in a dirt pile in the middle of Shakespeare's *Tempest*. He swears that his ghost will get revenge on a certain Czech!

The wolf trots up to the strange head in the ground. Shea lets out a fierce-sounding bark. The animal stops in its tracks. Shea doesn't know if he can cast any kind of spell with only the verbal elements at his command, but this is certainly the time to find out. What was it Chalmers said when he changed Votsy back from a werewolf? Shea begins chanting:

"Wolf, wolf, wolf of the noble Bard,
    Wolf of Shakespeare;
  I conjure you from beneath the yard;
    Leave me, and disappear!"

Since his hands aren't available, Shea gestures wildly in the air with his nose. The

Section 27

animal stares at him for a moment, then turns and trots off between the trees the way it came! Shea sighs. Was that really magic, or only a bored and unhungry wolf? He is glad Chalmers wasn't around to witness the encounter.

At least the sudden rush of fear has made him forget how cold he is. Shea resumes his neck motions in an effort to free the top of his body from the earth. At length, his neck hurts so much he gives up struggling and stares miserably up into the trees.

"Harold? Is that you?" Suddenly before him is a red-bearded face with eyes where the mouth ought to be. He shakes his head and blinks.

"Belphebe! Thank God. Get me out of here!"

The fire crackles pleasantly, though Harold Shea is feeling anything but pleasant. It took Belphebe over an hour to dig him out of the ground, and he is just now beginning to warm up. And he has the world's worst headache. Nothing dug that hole; he was inserted into the earth magically. He looks at a dirt-encrusted sleeve and frowns. His pinstriped suit will never be the same.

"Be of good cheer, my husband," Belphebe says as she turns a fat rabbit on a stick over the fire. "Our supper is nearly done."

"Vaclav is a mauve Hereford wandering

Section 27

around loose. The book of symbols is gone. We're lost in a world we know nothing about, and us with no weapons!" grumbles Shea. "Why should I be of good cheer?"

Belphebe touches him on the cheek. "Meseems you do forget you are not alone, my dearest."

Even without salt, the rabbit is the best meal he has eaten in recent memory. Belphebe isn't happy with her new bow, but it is good enough, thinks Shea. The sun sets and the air grows cooler. They drag several large branches together to stoke up the fire. Belphebe takes the first watch, and Shea is soon asleep with his head in her lap.

Turn to section 21.

28

They set out in the dark of early morning. Bitter-Root flits silently before them. Shea brings up the rear, stumbling along and feeling his way, but clinging tenaciously to the unicorn's tail. It is impossible to see much other than the animal's white rump. They travel uphill along the stream for some time. Twice, Shea loses his footing and nearly falls into the stream. The second time, he yanks so hard on the unicorn's tail that it almost throws Belphebe. From then on, the beast looks back at him angrily at the slightest tug.

Just as the purple light of dawn breaks over the treetops, they turn from the stream and head through a narrow, tree-covered valley. It is moist with dew and densely grown ferns, and the air is filled with a pleasant, musty odor. Shea looks ahead and notices two globes of amber light floating next to Bitter-Root, who hovers just above the trail.

The trees and ferns begin to close in. The grass underfoot gives way to wet stone. The unicorn comes to a sudden stop. Shea, who has let go of its tail, is busy taking in the

Section 28

sights and bumps into the rear of the beast. It responds by trying to nail Shea with its horn, but he dodges in the nick of time.

Bitter-Root is now surrounded by several mysterious floating balls of colored light. She turns and speaks: "See'st thou here, this is the mouth of our cell, and these"—indicating the floating lights—"are my fairy friends. The unicorn will come no farther. Pray dismount, Belphebe."

His wife hops off the unicorn in one graceful motion and takes the beast's head in her arms, whispering something into its ear. When she lets go, the animal eyes Shea warily and walks slowly around him. Safely past Harold, the unicorn shakes its head, snorts contemptuously, and bounds off the way they came.

Turn to section 16.

Section 29

* 29 *

Everything goes black. Shea's last thoughts are of Belphebe. He feels sad that he has let her down. . . .

The black turns to foggy gray and then becomes a whirlpool of white light into which he is falling.

Voices punctuate the fog.

"I think he's going to make it!"

Shea opens his eyes and finds himself staring into those of Duke Astolph, and by his side stands Merlin. They both have grave expressions on their faces, which turn to smiles when he looks up. Astolph is another interplanar wizard, though reared in a different time and place, who once saved Belphebe's life during Shea's visit to the Furioso.

The duke puts a gentle hand on Harold's forehead. "I say, old boy, that was a close one, eh wot? You American gangsters are tough birds! It was a bit of luck that brought your body here to the Sphinx Club. Without Merlin's help, I don't think I could have saved you!"

Shea can scarcely believe it. He is alive and well, and in London, of all places. Be-

Section 29

fore he can say a word, the duke continues, "We'll be sending you back to Hollywood..."

"Ohio!" interrupts Shea.

"Ohio," the duke goes on, "and next time be more careful."

Merlin holds out a thin hand and motions discreetly.

Harold Shea has lost one of his nine lives.

If you wish to try again, go back to section 1.

Section 30

* 30 *

Two of the goblins rush at Shea, while the others head for Belphebe. Harold ducks, eluding a swinging goblin club. As he rises, he delivers a roundhouse punch to the goblin's face and it falls to the ground, dropping its weapon. As he bends to grab the club, Shea feels the swish of another club passing over the top of his head. The goblin curses.

Meanwhile, Belphebe has stuffed the torch into the face of one goblin and is running around the cave with another in hot pursuit. Shea brings his club up butt first and smashes it into the jaw of his adversary, who falls to the ground moaning.

Just then, Shea catches a glancing blow to his shoulder, which spins him around. It is the goblin Belphebe has blinded with the torch. Shea takes aim and hits it square on the head. The goblin drops to its knees and falls over backward.

Belphebe runs in front of him with a monster hard on her heels. Shea sticks out his foot and trips the goblin who is trying to club his wife. It snarls, reaches over, and pulls Shea's legs out from under him. A wrestling match quickly develops between

Section 30

them, but Harold has the advantage of more than sixty pounds over the monster. They roll around on the clay floor, grunting and snorting. Shea gets his opponent in a vicious full nelson and snaps the poor creature's neck.

Harold looks around. There are no more goblins. "Nice work, kid!" he says in a breathless whisper to Belphebe.

"Nay, to you goes the credit, husband!" She bends over him and dabs at a scrape on his forehead.

They walk back to the door, and Shea gives it a gentle shove. It swings open.

Turn to section 63.

Section 31

* **31** *

Belphebe leads on, stepping carefully over and around the debris that litters the floor. Shea observes that it looks like the remains of many meals . . . a goblin garbage pile. They enter a large chamber and circle around the side. The air in the room is foul. It smells like unwashed bodies.

Belphebe stops suddenly. A loud snore comes from the darkness. She lifts her torch higher. There on a large pile of straw are several sleeping goblins.

Roll 3 D6 and compare the result to Harold's Dexterity value.

If the total of the dice is the same as or lower than Harold's Dexterity, turn to section 93.

If the total is greater, turn to section 25.

* 32 *

The tunnel drops sharply for a while and runs in a straight line. Shea wonders when, if ever, he will find his way out of the place. He is pleased when the passageway levels off and he hears running water in the distance.

Turn to section 65.

Section 33

* 33 *

Shea has trouble keeping his eyes open against the buffeting downdrafts created by the creature's beating wings. What he wouldn't give for his trusty épée now! He musters all his strength and swings the club at the harpy's outstretched claw. The monster pulls back at the last moment, and Shea whirls around like a baseball player who has just swung at a bad pitch.

The harpy cackles, and before Shea can regain his balance, his face is buried in smelly feathers. Something whacks him on the back of his head, and the world becomes a shower of stars.

Roll 1 D6. The number rolled is the number of hit points of damage Harold receives from the attack of the harpy. Subtract this from the total on the record sheet.

Turn to section 27.

* 34 *

"Well then, it shall be sport," Pholantus says, ominously squinting several eyes. He snaps his fingers. "Ephesia, my toys!" One of the demon's ugly little helpers patters off. Shea doesn't like the look of this.

"Thy skill with the blade interests me. We shall test it. . . ." Shea winces. The helper returns, carrying two iron tridents. "Using my weapons, of course!" the demon continues. One of the tridents is thrust into Shea's hands.

DEMON
To hit Shea: 13   To be hit: 12   Hit points: 10
Damage per attack: (both using tridents) D6+1

After each round of this fight, Harold may try to escape. Roll 3 D6. If the result is the same as or lower than Harold's Dexterity value, turn to section 94. Otherwise the fight continues.

If Harold is victorious, turn to section 42.

If Harold is killed, turn to section 87.

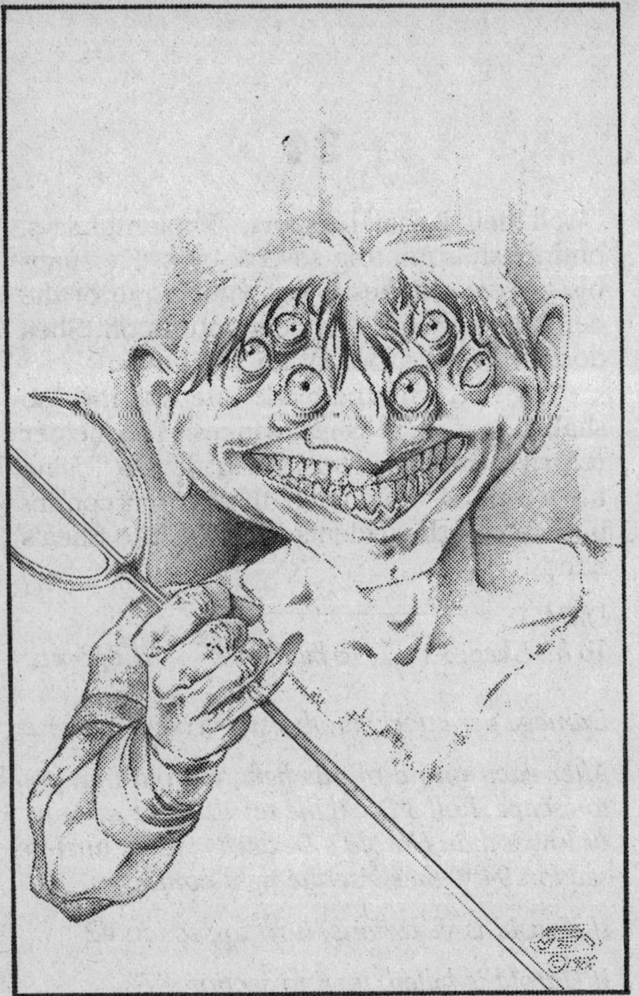

* 35 *

After sizing up the two goblins, Shea decides not to try any magical hanky-panky. Instead, he manages to lose gracefully, showering the winner with compliments. In the process, however, he shames the smaller goblin to such an extent that it challenges the larger one to another match.

"Good idea, boys," says Shea craftily. The big goblin, confident of a win, forgets about the bargain with Shea and starts playing. Harold recalls, from one of his earlier adventures, the way Heimdall had used magic to cheat in the cockroach races back in Surt's stronghold. Shea mumbles discreetly and makes subtle passes with his left hand. The large goblin's rocks consistently slide past the mark, while his opponent's stones always manage to stop on the highest score.

The result is inevitable. While the two goblins go at each other tooth and nail, Shea slips over to the column and unties their hapless friend.

"Many thanks," says the goblin as it falls to the ground. "I'm called Malovio." It extends a scaly green hand in friendship.

Section 35

"Harold Shea, here." He shakes the goblin's hand.

"Methinks we'd best be off before yon battle endeth!" says the goblin.

"But I'm hungry," complains Shea, "and they've got a pot of soup on. . . ."

"I, Malovio, can always find a meal. Let us away!" The goblin scoots off into the underbrush, and Shea follows.

Turn to section 88.

* 36 *

Fighting beside two additional copies of himself is a rare treat. Even before Shea finishes a thought about a possible stratagem, one of his duplicates is already executing it. In short order the two goblin guards are surrounded, disarmed, and knocked out with their own clubs. Shea is just about to congratulate himself by shaking his own hands when the two simulacrons vanish.

Good fun while it lasted, Shea thinks as he trots down the path that leads away from the cave. He reaches the spot where it switches back through a grove of dead pine trees and cuts off the trail. A horn sounds from the entrance to the caves. Shea struggles through the undergrowth, hurriedly putting distance between himself and his pursuers.

He runs at first, for what seems like an hour, crashing now and again into a clump of prickly thornbushes. Then his legs begin to ache and he slows to a steady walk. There has been no sign of the enemy since he left the path.

Turn to section 14.

* 37 *

Shea steps cautiously toward the sleeping drake. It looks peculiarly still . . . but then any creature who has been asleep for years would probably look that way. Just then, a gust of air blows the smoke from the torch into his eyes. Shea squints and his eyes water. For a moment, the image of the fire drake seems to fade. Uh oh! Shea concentrates on his disbelief and in a moment the whole illusion fades, revealing an empty room. There in front of him, only a step away, looms a large pit.

Shea mumbles, "There but for the grace of God . . ." He turns around and walks out the way he came.

Go to section 59.

Section 38

* 38 *

Two of the goblins rush at Shea, while the others head for Belphebe. Harold pulls out his rapier and lunges at the nearest goblin. The blade sinks into the creature's chest as it impales itself with its forward motion. The goblin falls to the ground, dropping its club. As Shea bends to remove his weapon, he feels the swish of another club passing over the top of his head. The goblin curses.

Meanwhile, Belphebe has stuffed her torch into the face of one goblin and is running around the cave with another in pursuit. Shea brings his rapier up butt first into the jaw of his adversary. It falls to the ground moaning.

Just then, Shea catches a glancing blow to his shoulder which spins him around. It is the goblin Belphebe blinded with the torch. Shea takes aim and, with a quick thrust, skewers the goblin on the tip of the rapier. The dying creature drops to its knees and falls over backward.

Belphebe runs in front of him with a monster hard on her heels. Shea sticks out his foot and trips the goblin who is trying to club his wife. It snarls, reaches over, and

Section 38

pulls Shea's legs out from under him. A wrestling match quickly develops between them, but Harold has the advantage of more than sixty pounds over the monster. They roll around on the clay floor, grunting and snorting. Shea gets his opponent in a vicious full nelson and snaps the poor creature's neck.

Harold looks around. There are no more goblins. "Nice work, kid!" he says in a breathless whisper to Belphebe.

"Nay, to your blade goes the credit, husband!" She bends over him and dabs at a scrape on his forehead.

They walk back to the door, and Shea gives it a gentle shove. It swings open.

Turn to section 63.

* 39 *

The moment Shea finishes the last words of the incantation, another of Sycorax's electric blue bolts crashes around them. The world turns gray, sand flies into Harold's face, and the entire beach erupts in a terrific explosion!

Roll 3 D6 and subtract that many points from Harold's hit point total.

If Harold is now dead, turn to section 29.

If Harold survives, turn to section 71.

Section 40

* **40** *

Belphebe helps her husband to his feet. "Harold," she implores, "you must do something, quickly!" He brushes the soot off his hands and face and tries the spell again with some minor changes. This time there is no clap of thunder, but the sootfall comes to an end.

A fine mist fills the air and turns to rain, which soon becomes an unbelievable downpour. It is almost as though they are standing under Niagara Falls. Shea grabs Belphebe's hand. He can hardly even see her. The ground on which they are standing becomes a river, and rushing water swirls around their legs. The spirits put their arms around Shea and Belphebe and pull them along to higher ground just as a wall of water, laden with logs and broken trees, washes across the valley.

Later, after the rain has stopped and the flash flood has subsided, a sodden Shea surveys the desolation below. The forest fire is out all right, and the goblins and the soot have been washed away. But so has half the countryside. The grassy field has turned into a litter-strewn, muddy swamp. Bitter-Root

Section 40

and Quamoclit are wringing out Belphebe's clothes.

"I think I got the decimal point wrong on that one," Shea says humbly.

"Ist the fire not drowned, and our enemies gone with the flood!" says Quamoclit.

"Yes, Harold," chimes Belphebe, "the day is ours!"

Shea keeps thinking of another line from Shakespeare: "The quality of mercy is not strain'd. . . ." Today it did more than droppeth gently from heaven upon the place beneath!

Turn to section 64.

* 41 *

Shea reaches carefully for Sycorax's staff. To his amazement, his hand passes through it, and the images of both the staff and the robe disappear. In place of the robe, a small glass bottle sits on the shelf. Shea removes his hand. The staff and robe reappear.

"Illusions," he whispers to Belphebe.

Return to section 63 and make a different choice.

* 42 *

Beads of sweat pop out on Shea's forehead before the fight even begins. His épée is one thing; this heavy iron trident is another. Pholantus circles around him threateningly. This is as much like fencing as football is like baseball . . . both sports require players and balls.

The demon lunges at him. Shea parries with a resounding clang and tries a riposte, but his weapon is so heavy that the demon easily deflects the effort. Pholantus advances and Shea gives ground. The sparring continues without result until Shea slips on a rock. As he struggles to regain his balance, the demon lunges and the tip of his trident pokes painfully into Shea's left arm.

Pholantus clucks with glee. The pain, however, makes Shea mad. Suddenly his weapon feels lighter, and he begins to wield it more like his épée. Barking like a mad dog, Harold advances, and it is all the demon can do to beat off the series of slow-motion one-twos Shea delivers with the heavy trident. Finally, Harold beats down his opponent's weapon and lunges in over the top, driving the three points deeply into the demon's chest.

Section 42

All of the demon's eyes open wide in amazement. "Fairly won!" gurgles Pholantus as he falls slowly to the ground. Shea turns quickly to face the ugly helpers, but they pay him no mind and run over to the demon, carrying something that looks like a bucket of water. They splash the liquid over their master, and steam rises from the body. Soon the wounds disappear, and Pholantus starts breathing again. He sits up with a broad smile on his face.

As he watches the demon's miraculous recovery, the helpers toss a bucket of liquid on Shea. "Hey! Watch it!" he yells, but his anger soon turns to joy as the holes in his arm magically disappear and a tingling feeling of wellness flows through his body.

Roll 2 D6. The result is the number of hit points restored to Harold. Add them to his total but do not exceed 17 hit points.

Pholantus steps forward, producing a reddish, glowing, translucent stone. "This is the DrakonStone," the demon intones. He offers it to Harold.

If Harold accepts, turn to section 89.

"Thanks, but no thanks," says Shea, refusing the stone.
"And I thank thee for the entertainment.

Section 42

However, thou hast kept me long enough from my business, so now farewell." Pholantus bows. "Ephesia will show you out." One of the ugly creatures leads Shea around the room and points to a small tunnel.

Turn to section 74.

Section 43

* **43** *

Shea turns and follows Malovio (at least he thinks it is the real Malovio) out of the main chamber, where the fight is still in full swing. The goblin surefootedly trots down the dimly lit tunnel and turns left into a small hole that Shea didn't even see. Inside, it is almost pitch dark till they come to a junction that is lit by a small torch. Shea reaches up and pulls it out of the wall.

Malovio motions wordlessly and they press on, deeper into the depths of the mountain. On and on through the black tunnels they go, and Shea begins to worry. Malovio trips on a rock and sits down to rub his knee. Shea looks up and down the corridor; there is no sign of life in any direction.

"How much farther do we have to go, Mal?" asks Shea, turning back to the goblin.

He freezes. The goblin is nowhere to be seen!

If Harold backtracks to look for Malovio, turn to section 73.

If Harold continues alone, turn to section 60.

* 44 *

The wolves snarl as Shea and Belphebe edge slowly around in front of them. The larger wolf lunges forward, only to receive a swift kick in the nose from Shea. Belphebe grabs a wooden stool and throws it at the second wolf, giving Harold time to pick up a small chair. In the background, Sycorax is screaming curses and baby Caliban sets up a hideous wail.

One of the wolves manages to nip Shea's ankle but pays dearly for its effort as Harold smashes the chair down on its head, knocking it cold. Seeing this, the other wolf begins to back away, still growling. Belphebe produces a dagger which she tosses across to Shea. A moment later, the wolf leaps for Harold's neck. He holds the dagger in front of him and rips the beast open with a deadly swipe. It falls to the ground with a dull thud.

By now, Sycorax is on her feet and seems to be making magic passes in the air as she prepares to cast some kind of spell. Whatever it is, Harold knows he will not like it.

Turn to section 69.

Section 45

* 45 *

Shea dives through an open space under the bush and scrambles to his feet. Ahead he can see some low-hanging evergreens. Their branches form such a tangle that it looks like a wall of solid green. Nothing can fly through that! He sprints forward, snatching a quick glance over his shoulder. The creature is just now coming over the top of the bush. With a look over his shoulder, Harold plows into the middle of the evergreens.

"Ouch!" he cries as the needles jab into his hands. Shea loses his grip on the book. It falls onto a springy branch and flies backward . . . directly into the monster's claw.

A twisted smile comes over the harpy's face. "I thank thee, dull fool!" it shrieks. With a flourish of wingbeats, it rises above the treetops and flaps off into the distance, laughing triumphantly.

"Well, that's that," Shea says miserably as he extracts himself from the trees. He pulls a pine cone out of his hair and looks around. No sign of the purple Polacek. He retraces his steps to the stream. He does not want to lose track of Belphebe too.

Section 45

Shea calls her name several times, but there is no answer. He spots his lighter and cigarettes on the ground and picks them up. Apparently the cow stepped on them, for the pack is mashed flat. Shea pulls out a flat cigarette and lights it with a sigh. No use getting too upset, he thinks, and he sits down.

The sun is low on the horizon, and the light breeze becomes cooler. There is still no sign of Belphebe. Shea gathers some branches and builds a roaring fire to make it easy for her to find him. Of course, something else might find him too. He finds another likely looking branch and begins to trim it. The finished product isn't beautiful, but he has a stout quarterstaff. He looks at it again in the firelight. Well . . . at least a club.

Darkness falls. Shea rolls a rock to the fire and sits down on it glumly. He is hungry, cold, and alone in a strange world. He begins seeing eyes staring at him from just beyond the light of the fire. At least he thinks they're eyes. No sooner does he blink and look again than the eyes disappear.

A tap on his shoulder startles him so badly that he falls backward off the rock. "Harold?"

"Belphebe!" he says with relief. "Where have you been?"

She holds up a fat brown rabbit. "I fin-

Section 45

ished my bow and went hunting. I see you have made a good fire." She looks around. "Where is Vaclav?"

As Belphebe roasts the rabbit on a stake over the fire, Shea relates the sad tale of the purple cow and his subsequent visit by the harpy. The rabbit proves delicious, as good a meal as she has ever cooked in the wild. When they finish eating, Shea drags up some additional wood for the fire. The eyes, whether real or imagined, are gone.

"Marry, good husband, certes I am pleased to be back in the wood," Belphebe says as she smiles at her husband. She begins to hum a tune she learned in Faerie, and Shea is soon fast asleep with his head in her lap.

Turn to section 21.

* 46 *

The fight with the wolves is more one of position and bluff than action. Harold and Belphebe circle slowly, and the wolves growl menacingly and match each step they take. One lunges, and Shea dodges nimbly to the right. Belphebe lashes out at the other wolf with a dagger and it quickly retreats. Harold blinks as he notices that they are now between the wolves and the door.

He nudges Belphebe with his elbow and motions with his eyes toward the door. She smiles to show her understanding. They back carefully till he has his hand against the wood. Then with a rush, Belphebe turns and darts out with Shea at her side.

Turn to section 69.

Section 47

* **47** *

Shea wakes with a start as a pair of goblins heft the pole to which he is tied onto their shoulders. Numb with pain and dizzy from lack of sleep, the events of the morning are all a blur. He vaguely remembers being carried bumpily along a trail during a heavy drizzle.

By noon he is painfully awake, swinging back and forth with the gait of his bearers, who have yet to stop for a rest. The trail leads steeply uphill. He cranes his head and sees that they are climbing the side of a still-smoking volcano. Suddenly they stop, and there is a brief discussion that he is unable to hear. Moments later they resume the march and soon enter a cold, dark lava cave.

The goblins carry Shea down a long, sloping corridor lit by an occasional torch. They stop again and are challenged.

"Who goes there?"

"We got one for the dungeon!"

"Be it large or small?"

"It's a big one!" There is a grunt and some clanking of keys. Someone or something slashes the ropes that hold his feet and hands

Section 47

to the pole, and Shea crashes to the floor. The pain of the fall is lost to him as he rejoices in the ache of circulation returning to his numbed hands and feet. He hears a door creak open.

"This'n will do!" Shea is dragged across the floor and ignominiously dumped into a pitch black cell. As the door slams shut, he struggles to a sitting position and pulls off his shoes to rub some life into his long-dead dogs. Shea looks around. Other than a faint yellow light shining through the hole in the door, he can see nothing, yet he has the curious feeling that he is not alone in the room.

He feels something breathing over his shoulder! He whirls around, and in so doing clips a goblin who is standing behind him on the chin with his elbow.

"Owww!" moans the goblin as it tumbles backward. "There's a fine way to treat a fellow prisoner." Shea's eyes adjust to the dark, and he can see his bug-eyed companion sitting on a pile of straw rubbing its chin.

"Sorry," says Shea, "but you shouldn't sneak up on me like that." He stands up; his legs are more than a little wobbly. "So where the hell are we?"

"We're in the dungeon of Firemount," answers the goblin. "You must be from afar. Never have I seen a man thrown here."

Section 47

Shea sits down next to the goblin. "You're right about that; I certainly came from far away."

The goblin extends a hand to Shea. "I'm called Malovio."

"Harold Shea, late of Ohio. What's your beef here?"

"I am branded a malingerer," Malovio answers, "but in truth, I am but an independent sort. Before that witch Sycorax, our life on this isle was full-easy. In Firemount we lived, and served the great drake, who was little enough trouble. Yet now, we are but stevedores and whipping-boys."

So the goblins aren't too fond of the witch either, muses Shea.

"Now lead I the renegade life, and 'tisn't an easy trip," complains Malovio.

"Who is this great drake?" asks Shea, seeing a potential ally.

"At the root of the Firemount now sleeps a mighty fire drake, a hot and fiery thing, yet Sycorax accurst it and full seven years hath it slept." Malovio sighs sadly. "And now slaves we are. The life of a goblin is not easy."

Shea's stomach gurgles with emptiness. "When's feeding time? I'm starving."

"Soon, but the slop served up is dog-bait," Malovio answers cynically.

Later, there is a rap on the door and a fat hand passes a bucket of swill through the

Section 47

hole. Shea can hardly see what it is for lack of light but it smells like old sauerkraut. Malovio passes on supper, and Harold greedily cleans out the container.

Shea belches. "Now I can think. How do we get out of here?"

"We don't; nobody does. Here we stay till we meet our ends," the goblin says glumly.

Shea was in a fix like this before. There is always a way out. He hasn't met or even seen his jailors, so bribing them might be a problem. He needs a quick out. Shea paces back and forth in the dark, narrow space, deep in thought. He glances at Malovio, who is scratching the dirt aimlessly with a straw. That's it! Simulacrons, just like the ones Lemminkainen made of him in the Kalevala!

Shea puts Malovio to work and soon they have assembled a collection of crude straw dolls. Shea reaches through the hole in the door and carefully arranges them on the ground outside the cell. He tries to recall the sound magic that the Elk of Hiisi used so successfully once before. He begins singing in a low voice and makes passes with his hands. Nothing happens.

"Is aught amiss?" asks the goblin.

"I'm not sure," Shea answers with a frown. He tries the passes again, this time reciting the words in verse instead of singing them.

Section 47

"What ho!" yelps the goblin. One by one, out in the passageway, the little dolls begin changing into life-sized replicas of Shea and Malovio.

"Identical copies of us," Shea remarks proudly. The replicas immediately spring into action. There is a cry and a thump followed by jingling keys. Two Malovios appear grinning at the door and promptly unlock it.

"Let's get out of here!" says Shea. "Do you know the way?"

"Certes, this is my home!" the goblin replies as he scoots out the door. All is pandemonium in the dungeon as the simulacrons of Shea and Malovio dash about unlocking cells, and the prisoners rush out to freedom. The original Malovio leads Shea through an open door and into a larger passageway where a group of goblin guards are being overwhelmed by a crowd of Sheas and Malovios. Shea can see the light of day at the far end of the tunnel, and he starts in that direction.

Malovio grabs his arm. "Too dangerous! Follow me, I know secret ways."

If Shea leaves Malovio and goes out the main entrance, turn to section 10.

If Shea follows Malovio, turn to section 43.

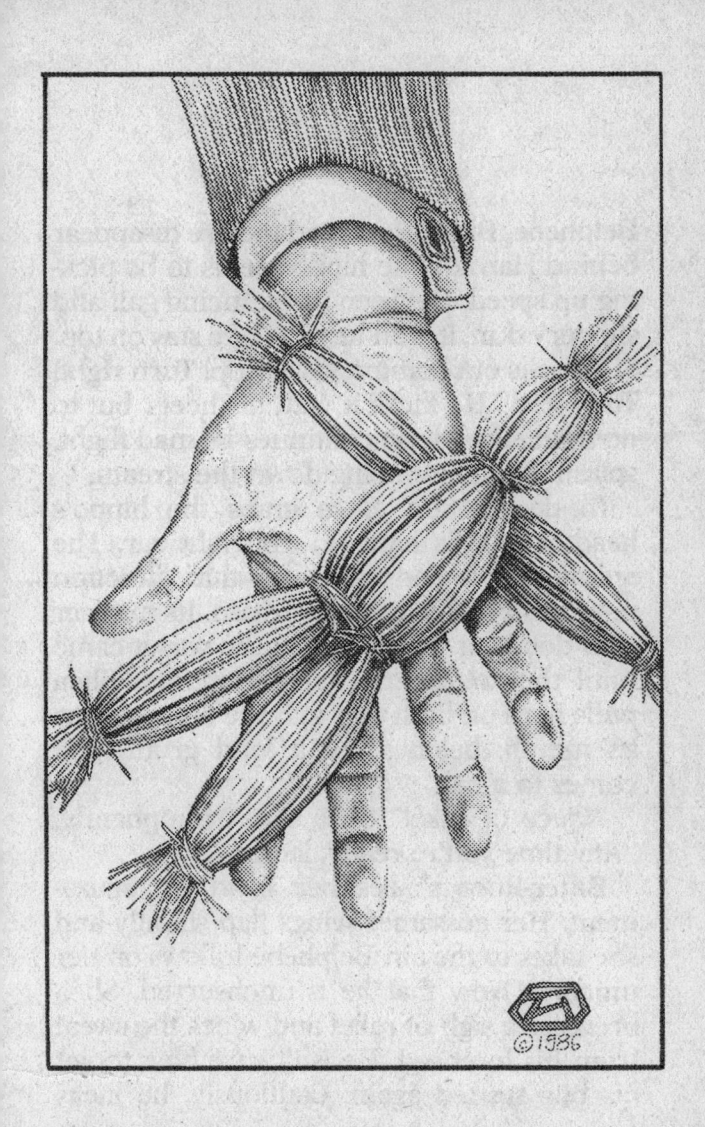
©1986

* 48 *

Belphebe, Bitter-Root, and the fire disappear behind Harold. The hippo seems to be picking up speed. Between its bouncing gait and slippery skin, it is all he can do to stay on top. Shea yells out commands: "Stop! Turn right! Turn left!" He kicks it with his heels, but to no avail. The hippo continues its mad flight, splashing and jouncing down the stream.

In desperation, Shea grabs the hippo's head and pulls hard on the right ear. The animal slows and circles in that direction until it is pointed back upstream. Its manner now docile, it waddles back the way it came until they reach the dying campfire. Shea pulls hard on both ears and the hippo opens its mouth, belches out a loud grunt, and comes to a halt.

"Piece of cake!" Shea says triumphantly. "Any time you're ready, ladies."

Bitter-Root shakes her head in amazement. Her gossamer wings flap silently and she takes to the air. Belphebe follows on her unicorn. Now that he is unobserved, Shea breathes a sigh of relief and wipes the sweat from his forehead. He isn't sure how to get his bus started again. Cautiously, he kicks

Section 48

the immense creature with his heels. The hippo comes to life and plods slowly after the unicorn.

They are traveling in the dark of early morning, and Shea can barely make out the ghostly forms of his companions in the weak starlight that filters through the trees. Fortunately, the hippo seems to be dogging the unicorn's steps and requires no steering at all.

They work their way uphill, following the stream for some time. At least Belphebe's mount and Bitter-Root stay alongside the stream. Whenever possible, the hippo prefers to splash noisily through the water, soaking Shea from the waist down.

Just as the purple light of dawn can be seen through the tops of the trees, they turn from the stream and head into a narrow, tree-covered valley. It is moist and overgrown with ferns, and the air is filled with a pleasant, musty odor. Shea notices that Bitter-Root has been joined by two globes of amber light that are floating along beside her.

The foliage closes in around them, leaving barely enough room on the trail for his wide-bodied mount. Soon, however, the vegetation gives way to rock and the trail widens. The procession comes to a halt, and the hippo grunts restively.

Bitter-Root is now surrounded by several

Section 48

mysterious floating balls of colored light. She turns and speaks: "See'st thou here, this is the mouth of our cell, and these"—indicating the lights—"are my fairy friends. Your animals will come no farther. Pray dismount and release them."

Belphebe hops down from the unicorn in one graceful motion. Shea slides off the hippo clumsily but manages to land on both feet. Belphebe is whispering into the unicorn's ear. Shea slaps his river horse on the rump and says, "Farewell, Horatio!" The beast lets out a series of low bleats and waddles off into the morning. The unicorn circles cautiously around Shea and trots off after the hippo.

Turn to section 16.

* 49 *

In a quiet whisper, Shea begins to chant:

"Beast of fire, whose council you keep,
    Fiend of Lord Surt, from under whose eyes,
I bid thee awaken, from Sycorax's sleep,
    Unto my command, now serve me. . . . Arise!"

Shea falls silent. For a moment nothing happens. Then the great mound that is the fire drake rises and falls in a great deep sigh. Years of accumulated rocks and dust fall off the top of the beast. Two glowing orange eyes pop open and stare malevolently into Shea's soul.

Its mouth opens in a hideous roar followed by a searing blast of flames that bounce off the walls and roll around and past Shea.

Roll 1 D6. The number rolled is the number of hit points of damage Shea suffers from the fire-breath. Subtract this number from the total on his record sheet.

Section 49
If Harold dies, turn to section 29.

If Harold survives, turn to section 90.

* 50 *

Belphebe dashes out into the dim light of evening, with Shea right behind her.

"Votsy, Snag!" he yells, but there is no answer. He can hear a great clamor from the cave behind them. They turn to run up the hill to where the brooms are hidden, but the air before them begins to blur, and a male spirit materializes before their eyes. It speaks two strange words and the ground on which Shea and Belphebe are standing turns to slime. They sink up to their knees, and the spirit laughs menacingly. It is the same laugh Shea heard when he met the harpy.

"Ariel," Shea says quickly as Sycorax appears at the entrance of the cave, "you gotta let us go!"

"Kill them!" commands the witch.

Shea reaches into his pocket and produces the tiny lock of hair that Bitter-Root gave him. "See this," he says in desperation. "Bitter-Root wants you back. You don't work for this damned witch!"

A look of obvious consternation comes over the spirit's face. Suddenly Shea and Belphebe are once again standing on solid ground. Harold grabs his wife's hand and

Section 50

pulls her into the bushes. The witch issues a volley of curses and shoots a lightning bolt at Ariel, who calmly dodges the fiery blast. Amid the turmoil, a crowd of ugly green goblins begin pouring out of the mouth of the cave.

"Let's get to the brooms!" Shea yells as he and Belphebe scramble through the thorns to the top of the hill. Not far behind, a small army of goblins follows. At the top of the hill, they find both brooms and Belphebe's bow, but there is no sign of Polacek or Snag. They quickly mount a broom, and Shea hurriedly chants the flight commands.

The two shoot into the air mere seconds ahead of the aroused goblins, and Shea banks into a slow turn. As they circle overhead, Belphebe puts arrow to bow and dispatches one monster after another. Shea searches for Polacek and Snag, but they are nowhere to be seen.

On the next pass over the hilltop, they are met by a shower of rocks thrown into the air by the surviving goblins. One rock clips Shea on the head and he sees the proverbial stars.

The next thing he knows, Shea is bound tightly hand and foot and hangs upside down from a long pole carried by a group of goblins. He cranes his aching head for a better look. All he can see is a procession of the ugly creatures marching along a rocky trail. It still seems to be evening and the sky is overcast. There is no sign of Belphebe.

Section 50

His arms are numb, and his head throbs painfully. This is a fine mess to be in.

Remove all items but the cigarette lighter from Harold's list of possessions.

The goblins march on in the growing dark, and Shea endures the pain until, at last, they stop for the night. They drop him roughly to the ground, still tied to the pole. At least it eases the pressure and allows a little blood to circulate into his extremities.

He turns his attention to the camp. There is a good deal of shouting going on. The dispute is over the lack of fire. Everything is still damp from the storm, and none of the goblins can start a fire.

Shea's elbow brushes against his pocket. . . . They haven't taken his lighter! Maybe he can put one over on these bozos.

If Shea tries to outwit a goblin and attempts to escape, roll 3 D6. Compare the result to Harold's Charisma value.

If the total of the dice is the same as or less than Harold's Charisma, turn to section 26.

If the total is higher than Harold's Charisma, turn to section 15.

If Harold doesn't try to escape, turn to section 47.

Section 51

* 51 *

Shea throws his club at the monster, grabs the book, and makes a dash for the woods. The fleeing cow has cleared a path that Harold gladly follows, hoping the trees will interfere with the flying monster. There is little undergrowth to slow Shea down, but the ground is uneven and littered with fallen trees. He runs clumsily down the rude path and leaps over a dead tree trunk. He turns left abruptly and dodges behind a large bush. The harpy is hot on his trail, beating its wings and hissing loudly. It is having absolutely no trouble negotiating the branches.

Roll 3 D6 and compare the total to Harold's Dexterity value.

If the total of the dice is the same as or lower than Harold's Dexterity, turn to section 45.

If the total is greater, turn to section 7.

* 52 *

Shea reaches up to the shelf and takes the small green vial in his hand. The scrawl on the side catches the light of the torch, and he is able to make out a word that seems to say "Health."

Belphebe reads it aloud and whispers, "An elixir with healing properties?"

"I think so," answers Harold, "but I can't be sure. . . . "

Add the potion to the list of Harold's possessions.

If at any time, including now, Harold drinks this potion, turn to section 70 (note this). Or you may have Harold drink the potion instead of attacking during his round of any combat.

Return to section 63 and make a different decision.

* 53 *

The large goblin takes a swing at Shea, who ducks and then puts up his dukes. So it is to be a boxing match. Well, boxing is a lot like fencing, and Harold Shea is a master. Using fancy footwork, he dances around his slow-witted opponent. Shea slips in several punches, adding to the goblin's fury. The other goblin, Gretio, seems quite content to stay in the background and only once makes an effort to trip Harold. Shea laughs, letting his guard down. At that moment, the big one lands a fist square on Shea's jaw, and he sees stars for a moment.

Now he is angry. Feeling like the Brown Bomber, Joe Louis, Shea takes the fight to the enemy. He lands a stiff shot to the goblin's gut and then connects with a left jab followed by a right cross. The goblin wobbles and then crashes to the mat. Shea turns to face Gretio.

"C'mon, bub, you're next!" the champ says defiantly. Rather than fight, the goblin shrieks and runs off into the brambles. "Hey! What'sa matter, you a coward?" Shea taunts. He dances around a bit more and then comes back to reality.

Section 53

The upside-down goblin is yelling, "Lemme down!" Shea walks over and unties the unfortunate creature.

"Many thanks," says the goblin as it falls to the ground. "I'm called Malovio. That was an impressive display of fisticuffs." It extends a scaly green hand in friendship.

"Harold Shea here," Shea says as he shakes the goblin's hand.

"Methinks we'd best be off before Gretio returns with the companions!"

"But I'm hungry," complains Shea, "and they've got a pot of soup on. . . ."

"I, Malovio, can always find a meal. Let us away!" The goblin scoots off into the underbrush, and Shea follows.

Turn to section 88.

* 54 *

The cave opens into a large, brown-walled chamber. In the distance, Shea can hear the faint drip of water. Just ahead, there is a torch set into the wall. Belphebe turns to make sure Shea is at her side and takes his hand. He thinks briefly of Snag and Polacek and wonders what kind of trouble the Czech has gotten them into.

They continue deeper into the cave. Belphebe leads the way, almost on tiptoe, being careful not to make a sound. Shea can see goblin footprints in the mud. They duck under a low rock and round a corner. Belphebe tugs at his sleeve. There before them, revealed in the dim yellow light, is a large wooden door set into the wall.

Upon closer investigation, Shea can make out interlocked pentacles lightly painted on the boards. Shea leans against the door and shoves. It does not move. There is no handle and no hinges are visible.

"This must be the old witch's room," he whispers to Belphebe. "Give me a couple strands of your hair." He knows how to handle a door locked in this fashion.

Reaching into his pocket, Shea produces

Section 54

two flattened cigarettes and ties them together in the form of a cross with Belphebe's hair. He holds this up to the door and tries to remember the proper wording of the spell.

Shea is about to cast a spell to break into the witch's chamber. Roll 3 D6.

If the total of the dice is the same as or lower than Shea's Wisdom value, turn to section 80.

If the total is higher than his Wisdom value, turn to section 18.

Section 55

* **55** *

Shea finishes the last words of the incantation, and the world turns gray. Sand flies into Harold's face, and the entire beach erupts in a terrific explosion!

Turn to section 71.

* 56 *

The wolves snarl as Shea and Belphebe circle cautiously in front of them. Very slowly, Shea eases the rapier out of his belt. The larger wolf growls and slobbers, then lunges forward only to run itself onto the point of Shea's outstretched blade. Belphebe grabs a wooden stool and throws it at the other wolf, giving Harold time to free his rapier. In the background, Sycorax is screaming bloody murder and baby Caliban has set up a hideous wail.

The surviving wolf manages to dart in and nip Shea's ankle but pays dearly for its effort as Harold thrusts deftly with his blade, and the rapier plunges through the animal's body. The wolf falls to the ground with a thud.

By now, Sycorax is on her feet, making magic passes in the air preparatory to casting some kind of spell. It is definitely time to leave.

Turn to section 69.

Section 57

* 57 *

Shea picks his way through the terrible tangle of thornbushes as best he can and heads northwest. An occasional glimpse of the trail and goblin travelers tells him that he is still in danger. As the sky glows red with twilight, he can hear a large band of goblins somewhere nearby. Panic combines with hunger and indecision, and Shea begins to run.

He crashes through a particularly nasty growth of prickly bushes and then turns uphill. At the top of a low ridge, he pauses and glances behind him to see if any goblins are on his trail. He sees none, even though their voices are still quite audible.

Shea kneels down and crouches behind a small boulder. Unfortunately, the rock on which he chooses to kneel is loose and, before he knows it, he is tumbling head over heels down the far side of the hill, away from the goblins.

Subtract 1 from Shea's hit point total.

If Harold dies, turn to section 29.

Shea dusts himself off and crawls behind a rock. He watches the top of the ridge anx-

Section 57

iously, but no goblins come over the crest of the hill. When he is certain that he has escaped without notice, he decides that his best bet is to make another flying broom. But try as he might, he cannot find a bird feather in this desolate place. Night comes on slowly, and a thoroughly discouraged Harold Shea begins to clear a sleeping area.

He has just settled down to an uncomfortable night's rest with a rock poking him in the side when a flash of light catches his eye. He shakes his head and looks again and spots a familiar, glowing red ball atop the next hill. It is circling slowly. A fairy!

Shea stumbles rapidly up the hill. When he reaches the summit, the red fairy buzzes excitedly around his head and then starts off into the dark. Shea follows. The fairy leads him along a rough path. After climbing what seems like an endless procession of low hills, he is rewarded by the sight of several fairies hovering in the darkness.

Turn to section 61.

Section 58

* 58 *

The large goblin takes a swing at Shea, who ducks and then puts up his dukes. So it is to be a boxing match. Well, boxing is a lot like fencing, and Harold Shea is a master. Using fancy footwork, he dances around his slow-witted opponent. Shea slips in several punches, adding to the goblin's fury. The other goblin, Gretio, seems quite content to stay in the background and only once makes an effort to trip Harold. Shea laughs, letting his guard down. At that moment, the big goblin lands a fist square on Shea's jaw and rings his bell.

From then on, things go downhill. The goblin sends a stiff shot into Shea's gut, and he begins to think he is up against a green version of the Brown Bomber, Joe Louis. Shea dodges a mean uppercut, sticks out his foot, and sends his opponent crashing to the mat. It isn't Marquis of Queensberry, but Shea was losing.

Harold scampers off the forum and crashes into the bushes. The two goblins yell foul, then light out after him. The boxing match has turned into a footrace, and Harold's longer legs give him the advantage. He

Section 58

leads his pursuers on a wild chase around the ruins until, eventually, he loses them and cuts back to where it all began.

The upside-down goblin is yelling, "Lemme down!" Shea walks over and unties the creature.

"Many thanks," says the goblin as it falls to the ground. "I'm called Malovio. That was an impressive display." It extends a scaly green hand in friendship.

"Harold Shea here," Shea says as he shakes the goblin's hand.

"Methinks we'd best be off before Frath and Gretio return with the companions!"

"But I'm hungry," complains Shea, "and they've got a pot of soup on. . . ."

"I, Malovio, can always find a meal. Let us away!" The goblin scoots off into the underbrush, and Shea follows.

Turn to section 88.

Section 59

* 59 *

Shaking his head about Malovio. Shea walks down the corridor that he was advised not to take. The path winds steeply downward. The echoes of his footsteps make him keenly aware of the great size of the tunnel. Several minutes and many tiresome footsteps later, the cave opens into a vast chamber. The torch is too weak to light the far side, so he cautiously tiptoes across the room.

Shea blinks. A great black mass looms in front of him. What he first thinks is a rock wall is actually the enormous bulk of the sleeping fire drake. Quietly Shea backs away, then kneels down and constructs a rough model of the drake out of cinders.

Shea is about to cast a spell to take control of the fire drake. Roll 3 D6.

If the total rolled is the same as or lower than Shea's Wisdom value, turn to section 62.

If the total rolled is higher than his Wisdom value, turn to section 49.

* 60 *

Shea walks cautiously on. The cave is now eerily quiet. The turmoil in the dungeon can no longer be heard. The small torch he found provides enough light to see . . . but it also means he can be seen. The floor levels off abruptly, and the torchlight reveals three tunnels before him, each heading off in a different direction into the darkness.

Shea examines his possible choices. The tunnel to the left feels warm and the air smells strongly of sulphur. He walks across to the far side. There the air is stale and thick and holds the odor of death. The center tunnel is by far the most appealing, as the air smells clean, cool, and fresh.

If Harold takes the left tunnel, turn to section 76.

If Harold takes the right tunnel, turn to section 78.

If Harold takes the center tunnel, turn to section 17.

Section 61

* 61 *

Shea breaks into a run and notices that he is again in tall grass. More fairies appear, clustered around two human forms, one with wings, and . . . Belphebe!

They fly into each other's arms.

"Harold, darling, we have been searching for you everywhere!"

"I'm mighty glad to see you alive," Shea says, and he plants a kiss on her lips. They return to the spirit cave on the two-seater, with Belphebe in the pilot's seat. She has learned how to fly a broom in his absence and handles it much like she did the Shea Chevrolet. He wisely keeps his mouth shut.

Belphebe bathes Shea in a pool inside the cave, and the spirits give him a wine that tingles through his body and restores his strength. He sleeps like a log.

Roll 1 D6 and add the result to Harold's hit point total (do not exceed 17 total points).

At breakfast, Harold learns that Snag and Votsy are missing, as is the magic book.

Section 61

Then Quamoclit comes buzzing in excitedly. The witch and an army of goblins have marched into the spirit lands and have set a great fire which is rolling rapidly toward the spirit cave.

"Damn," Shea says angrily. "Sycorax must be upset over my escape."

"We must do something, Harold," says Belphebe. "Even without the book you are still a master of magic."

"In the face of Sycorax, I wouldn't be too sure," says Shea, but they mount their broom and, accompanied by the spirits, fly off to see what is afoot.

Cruising low over the treetops, they spot the fires and land in the field where they had first appeared on the island. The surrounding forests are all ablaze, and goblins are running to and fro with torches spreading the conflagration.

Shea puts his hand to his head trying to remember the spell he had used in the Kalavela to bring rain. Even though in that case it backfired and brought clouds of soot, he has to try; the forest fire before them is raging out of control. He makes several passes and begins to chant a few lines of rather poorly constructed poetry about April showers. He sang the spell in Finland, but spoken verse seems to work better in the world of Shakespeare.

Section 61

Roll 3 D6 and compare the result to Harold's Wisdom value.

If the total of the dice is the same as or lower than Harold's Wisdom, turn to section 8.

If the total is higher, turn to section 24.

* 62 *

In a quiet whisper, Shea begins to chant:

"Great beast of the fire, whose council you keep,
  Good friend of lord Surt, from under whose eyes,
I bid thee awaken, from Sycorax's sleep,
  Unto my command, now serve me. . . . Arise!"

Shea falls silent. For a moment, nothing happens. Then the great mound that is the fire drake rises and falls in a great deep sigh. Years of accumulated rocks and dust fall off the top of the beast. Two glowing orange eyes pop open and stare into Shea's soul.

He fully expects to be roasted by a blast of flame, but the giant drake rises slowly to its feet, stretches itself interminably, and walks calmly over to where Shea stands. He thanks his stars and climbs onto the creature's neck, which is no easy task. Shea settles comfortably between two large plates on its back and recites a further rhyme:

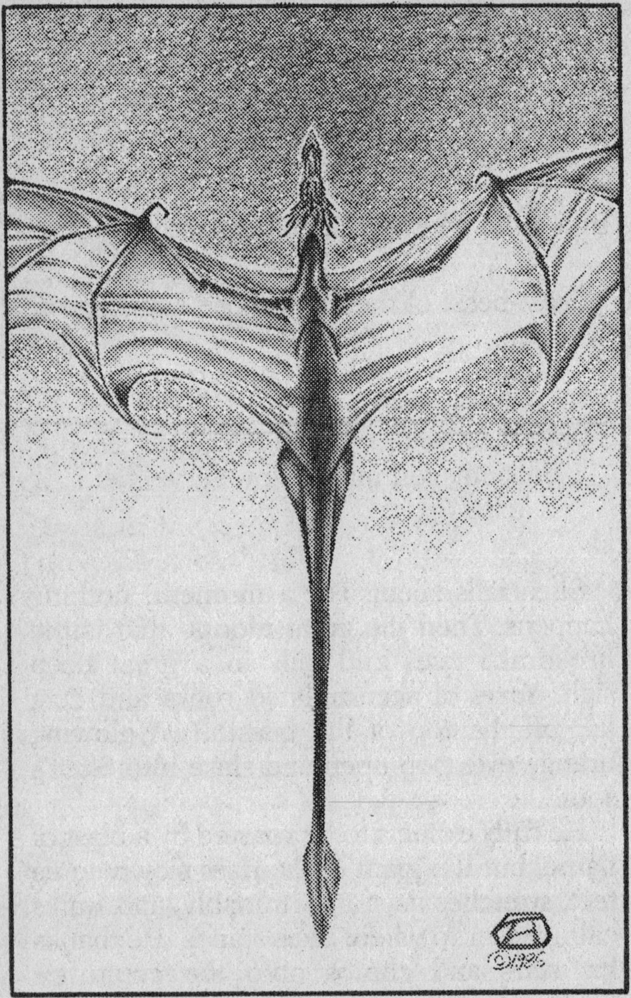

Section 62

"Onward, mighty steed, into battle we fly,
  To fame and to glory, our victory is
    nigh . . ."

Before Harold can finish, the drake lurches forward, rises from the cave floor, and zooms toward the entrance with alarming speed. Shea can't imagine how the thing flies with its monstrous wings in this confined space. He hangs on for dear life.

In a moment they flash out through the opening into the light of day, and Shea is temporarily blinded as his eyes adjust to the light. The great wings of the fire drake begin beating with a low, rhythmic murmur, and they rise swiftly above Firemount. Shea isn't sure how he controls the monster, but it is doing exactly what he wants. Can it be telepathic?

Shea tests his theory by thinking about flying up and over in a tight loop. He regrets the thought instantly as the drake swirls effortlessly over, with Shea hanging on by his fingernails. Satisfied that he is in control, Harold points his juggernaut in the direction of the battle.

Belphebe curses as a rock smashes into her shin. Ever since Harold mysteriously departed, she, Polacek, and Snag have been in control of the army of spirits, sailors, and

Section 62

fairies, and it hasn't worked any too well. Polacek keeps leafing through the magic book and attempts to cast spells which invariably fail or, worse, backfire and kill several of their own number.

Snag proves to be a natural leader, dividing his forces into platoons of fighting sailors who go into battle with no fear of death. Each time the forces of the witch make a move to outflank, Snag responds by sending in a counterattack that drives her minions back.

Sycorax is persistent, and she drives her army of goblins forward. Although Belphebe and her archers, and Snag and his sword- and spearmen, take a fearful toll of the enemy, the witch seems to have an endless supply of dark green, willing-to-die creatures. Snag is forced to give ground again.

The spirit cave is overwhelmed, and they retreat over the ridge to the next hill . . . and then to the next, and the next. A bolt from the witch strikes Quamoclit, and she is driven into the heart of a pine tree. Belphebe winces as she hears the spirit scream. The sailors retreat at a command from Snag, and all, including Belphebe, run at full speed over the last hill that stands between them and the sea. The huntress searches the sky in vain for a sign of her husband.

A brief respite is achieved when Polacek casts a spell that actually works. For several

Section 62

minutes, a large cloud of noxious yellow smoke pours out of a tree stump. As it drifts over the goblins, they reel back in agony.

"Phosgene," says Polacek, smiling. "It's an old trick of the Huns used in the First World War."

Belphebe looks at him with a puzzled expression. Harold told her of a world war, but she never heard of this. She is more concerned about the fact that there are only seven arrows left in her quiver, and the sailors who stand by her side all seem to have equally low supplies of missiles.

There is a sudden shout, and all faces look skyward. Coming over the crest of the hill is a monster of enormous proportions. Another of the witch's servants, no doubt. They are surely doomed. Belphebe puts her hand to her forehead and groans.

Polacek begins dancing up and down and shakes her. "It's Harold," he exclaims. Belphebe looks up in amazement and awe.

Shea is horrified to see the vast number of goblins that still swarm over the forests below. His heart sinks when he sees the spirit cave overrun. Is he too late? He banks to the left and swoops over the last row of hills.

There they are! He has arrived none too soon. The good guys have their backs to the wall. Well, here is where Harold Shea saves

Section 62

the day! He puts the fire drake into a sharp wingover and thinks about a stream of fire.

As his mount swoops in heavily from above, a blast of orange flame shoots out of its mouth, engulfing hundreds of unfortunate goblins. Shea grins as he pulls up and circles for another pass. A few more strokes like that and the witch will be out of business (and goblins).

He flies low over the army of sailors and can hear a cheer rising up from below. He spots Belphebe and waves triumphantly. The drake flies out over the sea and then circles back for the next attack. This time, Shea intends to roast Sycorax and end the battle once and for all. He catches sight of her red robe and aims the drake straight at her, thinking flamethrower thoughts.

Suddenly a bolt of electric blue light rises from where the witch stands and envelops Shea and his mount. The fire drake shudders. Its wings stop beating, and it veers off to the left. Shea finds himself spiraling to the ground aboard a dying bomber.

With a dreadful crash, the drake plows into a mass of trees, snapping them off like matchsticks. Shea is thrown brutally into the side of a sand dune. He lies there, stunned.

Subtract 1 hit point from the total on Harold's record sheet.

Section 62

If Harold dies, turn to section 29.

Shea struggles to get his breath. He is still alive, he thinks to himself. It could be worse. He rolls dizzily down to the base of the dune and sits, holding his spinning head in his hands, trying to orient himself. At last he sees Belphebe, jumping up and down and motioning to him. Shea struggles to his feet and staggers through a rain of goblin-thrown rocks to reach her side.

Turn to section 13.

Section 63

* 63 *

A dim red light shines out into the cave from within the room. Harold and Belphebe enter cautiously. Inside, Shea can see that the illumination comes from glowing coals, all that remains of a large fire that has been set in the center of the room. Arranged around the edges of the room is an assortment of crude wooden furniture, hanging tapestries, some shelves covered with assorted oddities, and a long, low bed on which lies... Sycorax! She is sleeping with her mouth open, snoring quietly.

Shea and Belphebe hold their breath as they edge around the walls of the room past the sleeping witch. Up close, the hag is even uglier than Shea imagined, and she doesn't smell any too good either. He notices a smaller, boxlike structure situated near the bed. A strange hissing noise comes from within. A quick look inside reveals a disgusting, sleeping baby that resembles a dead fish.

"Caliban," Shea whispers to his wife. She nods her agreement.

They go to the shelves and Harold examines them carefully without touching any of the objects they hold. The pentagram words are disabled, but there might easily be other,

Section 63

less visible, traps guarding the witch's possessions. Belphebe nudges Shea and points to Doc Chalmers' book of symbols. It is wedged in between several black leather-bound books. With a careful hand, Shea gently slides the magic book out from between the two moldy leather tomes. He opens it briefly; everything appears to be all right.

Slipping the book into his breast pocket, Shea continues his explorations. Nearby is a small mirror and a small green vial with some writing scratched on the side. At the far end of the shelf, Shea can see Sycorax's red robe, folded neatly, and leaning against it, her long crooked staff.

Beneath the shelves, Harold finds a cache of assorted weapons, mostly daggers, but a large axe with a sharply honed edge lies on top of the pile.

Belphebe spots the axe and whispers in Shea's ear, "An opportunity to end this struggle once and finally presents itself, Harold." She picks up the weapon and offers it to her husband.

If Harold tries to steal the small bottle, turn to section 52.

If Harold tries to swipe the staff and robe, turn to section 66.

If Harold takes the axe and tries to chop off Sycorax's head, turn to section 5.

* 64 *

Shea wades back into the mud and, with help from his companions, manages to pull the flying broom out of the muck. Most of its feathers are missing, and it is all he can do to get it to limp along a few feet above the ground as they fly back up the stream toward the spirit cave. The flood has done an efficient job of clearing the valley.

Belphebe nudges Shea and points at two figures mired in a sea of mud below. It is Votsy and Snag! The two men yell and wave as the broom and the spirits approach.

"Harold, Belphebe! You wouldn't believe the storm we just had!" says the Czech excitedly as Shea cautiously lands the broom on the mud. Polacek is trying to free a log apparatus that looks rather like an oxcart and is filled with round stones.

Belphebe laughs. "We would believe, Vaclav. Harold summoned the storm to put out a forest fire."

"Holy bejesus, don'cha think ya overdid it?" complains Polacek. "It nearly washed us away!"

"Where on earth have you been?" demands Shea. "You were supposed to wait for us outside the witch's cave!"

Section 64

"Hey, we waited. Then a bunch of goblins came along and Snag had to crack a few heads." The sailor looks up and smiles. "When we came back, all hell broke loose and the witch's guards were everywhere. So we laid low till dark and then sneaked back to where the brooms were hidden."

"There Pollychek found the book, too," adds Snag.

"You've got it?" Shea asks. The Rubber Czech pulls the volume out from under his coat.

"Safe and sound. Your broom was gone so I figured you must be all right. Then I had this idea." Polacek slaps the log device proudly. "We've got a whole army here!"

Belphebe's eyes light up. "You brought back the sailors from the beach!"

"You got it, Toots. And this truck used to fly, albeit slowly, till Harold washed us out with that flood."

Shea shakes his head in disbelief.

They spend the rest of the day digging out Polacek's truck and finally manage to get the load of sailors, in the form of rocks, safely inside the spirit cave. There is a heated debate between Polacek and Shea as to how and who will turn the stones back into men. The spirits sadly complain that the power of Sycorax is beyond them; their magic cannot help.

Shea places one of the stones in the center

Section 64

of a table and tries the sound magic used to raise simulacrons. When he finishes, there are two rocks on the table but no sailors. Polacek tries next, with one of the spells Chalmers intended to use to restore Florimel's human form. There is a puff of smoke, and the rock turns into a foot-long bullfrog.

Polacek bursts out laughing. "A fitting end for a man of the sea!" Snag grabs him by the throat. "Just kidding, just kidding, Snag. I won't do it again." They go to sleep that night in a cave full of rocks.

At breakfast, Shea stands up with a start. "Votsy! We are both right! We need to combine the verbal elements of the sound magic with the somatic elements of the spell you used . . . and watch the decimal point." They quickly set up another stone and together they make passes and chant. Their voices reach a crescendo, then, *WHUMP!*

A very startled, naked man appears on the tabletop. Belphebe and the spirits cheer. An assembly line is set up. Shea and Polacek convert the stones back to men, the spirits clothe them, and Snag and Belphebe arm and organize them. By evening the cave is packed with hundreds of ex-rock sailors.

"How many stones did you gather, Votsy?" Shea asks while they stop for some wine.

"I dunno, maybe a couple thousand."

At the end of the third day, the last stone has been turned. They even find the bullfrog,

Section 64

who proves to be a businessman from Venice. He is very grateful, just the same. The armed camp overflows the spirit cave and a tent city springs up on the hillside.

Belphebe sorts out the men most adept at archery and organizes a contingent of missile troops. The rest of the men are armed with assorted spears, swords, clubs, and even rocks. Most of the ships' passengers request assignment to the ambulance corps.

The four adventurers and the spirits hold a conference, trying to decide how best to use their army, when Bitter-Root flies in with disturbing news. The witch and her goblins are on the march again, and there are more goblins than anyone can believe.

By the time the ragtag sailor army is ready to march, the goblins have already crossed the mudflats and are coming up the valley, heading straight for the spirit cave. Shea and Belphebe fly a reconnaissance mission, and they too are shocked at the number of goblins.

"There must be ten thousand of them down there," Shea complains as they circle back to their lines.

"Our cause is just, Harold," says Belphebe reassuringly.

Snag has deployed the army in a wide arc across the valley, massing Belphebe's archers and his best spearmen behind the line as a reserve.

Section 64

As the goblin army approaches, a silence falls over the valley. Then a bolt of lightning from Sycorax crashes into a tree near Shea and the goblins rush forward. Just as their ranks reach the spirit army, Belphebe's archers fire a volley into the air. The goblin center disintegrates. On the two flanks, however, the armies come together and are soon locked in fearful melee.

Shea takes Belphebe up on the broom and cruises up and down the enemy line while she picks off goblin leaders with well-aimed shots. Sycorax soon catches on and starts popping lightning bolts at them. After a near-miss singes the feathers on their tail, Shea clears the skies and heads back to terra firma.

The press of the goblin army is overwhelming, and Snag orders a general fall-back. At this rate, it is apparent that the witch will soon drive them into the sea. Shea pulls Belphebe aside and tells her to continue the fight; he has a plan and will return. He holds her in his arms for a brief parting kiss and then flies off alone on his broom.

Shea stays low, whizzing over the treetops until he is out of sight of the goblin army, then turns south for Firemount. He isn't sure how he will do it, but he intends to enlist the aid of the fire drake mentioned by Malovio. As he cruises in for a landing outside of the volcano, the place seems mysteriously

Section 64

empty. Small wonder! Every able-bodied goblin has gone to war. A moan catches his ears as he searches the base of the mountain for an entrance.

Hanging upside down by a rope from a dead tree is Malovio. "In trouble again, no doubt," Shea mumbles as he cuts the hapless goblin down.

The goblin rubs its ankles. "Many thanks again, Harold. I refused to serve."

Shea asks directions to the fire drake.

"'Tis on the other side of the mountain," says the goblin.

Shea mounts the broom. The goblin eyes it with terror and backs up, babbling, "I must away. . . . " Harold grabs Malovio's arm and drags him aboard. The goblin wails as they fly rapidly around the base of the mountain. Suddenly Malovio points. Shea notes a large cave and eases the broom through the dark entrance.

"Thou woulds't strain our friendship!" complains the goblin as they dismount and hide the broom near the entrance.

"I'm sorry, old boy, but this is a life or death emergency. I have to find the fire drake," says Shea. He nudges Malovio with his elbow and the goblin leads on, deeper into the cavern.

They come to a deserted guard station and find a supply of weapons and torches. Each of them takes a torch. The cavern is wide and

Section 64

tall, large enough, Shea imagines, to pass the drake. They come to a place where the tunnel splits off in two directions.

Malovio becomes nervous and hops back and forth from one foot to the other. He will go no farther.

"Take the path to the left!" the goblin cries as he tosses away his torch and runs full speed back the way he has come. Shea starts after him, then changes his mind. He doesn't have time.

If Shea trusts Malovio and takes the left passage, turn to section 22.

If Shea ignores Malovio and takes the right passage, turn to section 59.

* 65 *

Shea picks up his pace. There is daylight shining into the cave up ahead. He comes to a long pool of crystal-clear water. To the left is a small waterfall and above that, daylight. That's what he wants! After a short struggle up some wet and slippery rocks, Shea returns to the world outside. He is glad to be out, but the scenery is depressing, nothing but dead trees and bramble bushes. He starts walking in what he hopes is a northerly direction.

Turn to section 14.

* 66 *

Shea declines the proffered axe and walks silently to the end of the shelves. He examines the staff and folded robe carefully and then reaches out.

Roll 3 D6 and compare the result to Harold's Dexterity value.

If the total of the dice is the same as or lower than Harold's Dexterity, turn to section 41.

If the total is greater, turn to section 84.

* 67 *

Shea creeps forward toward the center of the chamber. He notices a pile of cinders that will be useful for casting the spell he has in mind. As he steps over a large rock, the world around him suddenly begins spinning. He experiences a falling sensation. Then . . . thud! He crashes to the bottom of a shallow pit.

Subtract one hit point from the total on Harold's record sheet.

If Harold dies, turn to section 29.

His nerves badly jangled, Shea climbs quickly to his feet, hoping the noise of his fall hasn't awakened the fire drake. Why didn't he see this hole in the ground before? It is certainly large enough! Slowly Shea peers over the edge of the pit at what should have been the sleeping drake, but it is nothing but a solid mass of hardened lava. An illusion! Shea curses Malovio and stomps out the way he came in.

Turn to section 59.

Section 68

* 68 *

Shea stands behind the sarcophagus as the door smashes open. In rushes an angry goblin, yelling oaths and cursing Shea for defiling his dead. Another one follows.

FIVE GOBLINS
To hit Shea: 14   To be hit: 11   Hit points: 3 each
Damage with clubs: D6 (Shea uses the club that was on the table.)

The goblins enter the room one at a time. After each round of combat, one additional goblin will be attacking Shea until all five have entered the room.

After each round of this fight, Harold may try to escape. Roll 3 D6. If the result is the same as or lower than Harold's Dexterity value, turn to section 92.

If the result is higher, the fight continues.

If Harold wins the fight, turn to section 81.

If Harold is killed, turn to section 29.

* 69 *

Shea grabs Belphebe by the hand and dashes through the large wooden door. As they pass, he reaches out and pulls it shut. It slams heavily behind them, throwing the cave into almost total darkness.

Shea pauses. Belphebe pulls him forward, hissing, "This way, Harold!" and they stumble along in the dark. She pushes his head down as they duck under a low rock. Once around the next corner, he can see a dim light ahead. They run at full speed past some broken statues and then struggle uphill toward the daylight that beckons.

Turn to section 50.

* 70 *

Shea pulls the wax seal off the top of the small vial. Expecting the worst, he takes a quick sniff and is surprised by the pleasant scent of fresh flowers. Now is the moment. Drinking this stuff could heal him or it could kill him. Shea gulps it down in once quick swallow. Instantly, a tingle of relief surges through his body, and Shea drops the vial to the ground.

The vial contains a potion of healing. Roll 2 D6. The total of these dice is the number of hit points restored to Harold Shea. Add these to his total on the record sheet. Remember that his total hit points may not exceed 17. Any extra points of healing are lost. Remove the vial from Harold's list of possessions.

Return to whatever section you were in and continue the adventure.

* 71 *

The smoke clears, revealing a scene of utter serenity. Gone are the piles of dead bodies, the goblins, the sailors, the witch, and the fire drake. Three bodies lie sprawled on the beach behind some clumps of grass. One of them moves.

Shea groans and pushes himself up on his elbows for a look around. Nothing is left! He reaches over and touches Belphebe, who is just coming around, and sees Polacek, who is laying on his back mumbling something. What happened? Why aren't they in Ohio?

Out on the beach he sees a bearded man pulling a small boat ashore. With him is a little girl. The man looks around at the pristine beach and says to the girl, "What a quiet and unspoil'd place is this. . . . "

Shea groans. The man tosses his bundles on the beach and walks inland, holding the girl's hand. Shea nudges Vaclav, who has crawled over to his side and is also watching.

"There's your Miranda, Votsy. A five year old! And that man's Prospero, her father. We're in the same continuum, but farther along the timeline. The boat they were cast adrift in has just come ashore."

Section 71

Prospero stops suddenly and bends down. He picks up a book and studies it with interest.

"Our book," whispers Vaclav. Prospero begins bobbing back and forth as he reads, motioning with his hands. He is reciting something which Shea can't quite understand. Suddenly the world around them turns gray and begins to spin. *PMFT!*

A whoosh of air makes the curtains dance. Shea, Belphebe, and Polacek find themselves lying on the stage at the theater. The seats are empty save for one man, who begins to clap slowly. It is Reed Chalmers.

Shea pulls Belphebe into his arms.

"Hey, Doc," says Polacek as he sits up, "I bet you didn't know that one of those books in Prospero's library came from the Garaden Institute, right here in Ohio!"

THE END

* 72 *

"Nobody move," whispers Shea. "You'll get your chance to fight soon enough, Snag. We're trying to sneak in, not fight our way through."

Snag grits his teeth. The two goblins continue their debate and eventually wander off down the other side of the hill. Snag finishes eating and takes the watch while Belphebe eats. Somehow, Polacek manages to consume most of the wine.

The brooms are stashed under a clump of brown bushes on top of the hill. Harold persuades Belphebe to leave her longbow as well, as it is unsuited to quick travel in the tight passages of a cave. The storm has abated, though it still drizzles as they make their way down the slope in the gathering dusk of evening.

The main entrance to the witch's cave is a gaping hole in the side of the hill. The four hide behind a log as a group of goblins come out and walk on down the path. After a brief discussion, Polacek happily agrees to stand watch at the entrance with Snag, while Shea and Belphebe go in to steal the magic book.

Section 72

"What do we do if you guys don't come out?" asks the Czech.

"We rescue them," Snag says curtly.

"My thoughts, exactly," adds Shea. "Give us till morning, then do something if we're not back."

They wait a few more minutes. No more goblins appear. Belphebe leads the way to the entrance, where she finds a convenient supply of crude torches. Shea's lighter provides fire, and they set off into the cool darkness.

They creep in silently, keeping to one side of the massive cave. The floor is firm damp clay and is relatively level. Soon, the walls and the ceiling begin to close around them and the cave begins sloping downward. The daylight fades behind them.

The guards must all have the day off, Shea thinks to himself as they work their way deeper into the witch's lair without meeting so much as a mouse. But then, what do they have to guard against? The spirits are afraid to come near this place, and the sailors have all been turned into stones. Maybe there aren't any guards at all.

They round a curve. Ahead, the cave splits off into two directions. Some crumbling Roman statues line one passage. The other is filled with bones and assorted garbage. Both ways look well used.

Section 72

If Harold and Belphebe take the statue path, turn to section 6.

If they take the littered path, turn to section 31.

* 73 *

Shea turns around and works his way back up the tunnel in the dim torchlight. Even though the ground is covered with tiny cinders, he can only see one set of footprints ... his own. He rounds a corner and steps gingerly over a sharp slab of rock, and is faced with two tunnels that go off in opposite directions. The floor is solid rock, and he can see no footprints.

Shea shakes his head in disgust, cursing the stupid goblin. He hears the faintest of noises coming down one of the tunnels and turns in an effort to locate the sound. Goblin guards! So much for finding Malovio, he thinks to himself as he climbs back over the sharp rock and trots back down the dark tunnel.

Turn to section 60.

* 74 *

Shea steps into the tunnel. It is smaller than he first thought, and he bends down to get through the entrance. He takes two short steps and feels himself slipping on the glassy smooth floor. He reaches out, desperately seeking a handhold, but the walls are smooth and slick as well. He hits the slanting floor with a thud and begins to slide helplessly downhill.

At first the incline is not too steep, and Shea tries to arrest his downward progress by wedging the soles of his shoes flat against the slippery floor. It doesn't work. He begins to pick up speed. He tries stretching his hands and feet to opposite sides, but can create no friction. The surface slides past like ice.

A sudden increase in the angle and speed of his descent brings butterflies to Shea's stomach, and soon he is zooming at an alarming rate almost straight down in the dark. He searches his mind, desperately trying to think of some kind of spell that will slow him down or allow him to land softly, but all he can think of is being dashed on a pile of sharp rocks.

Section 74

As quickly as it sloped down, the slide levels out, pressing Shea against the floor as it curves back. He scoots a few hundred more feet and comes gently to a stop in a pile of black sand. There is light coming from somewhere up ahead, and Shea can hear the sound of running water. The air is the freshest he has smelled since entering this dank place. He climbs to his feet and walks cautiously forward.

Turn to section 65.

* 75 *

As he walks up the side passage, Shea catches the scent of smoke in the air. He is surprised to encounter a rough-hewn stairway, which he climbs. There is a room at the top of the stairs. Torchlight reveals a huge iron cauldron in the center, bubbling over glowing charcoal. He glances around suspiciously. Nobody is home.

Shea walks over to the pot. As he circles around it, he sees raised letters on the side:

"Double . . . Double . . . Toil . . . and . . ."

He turns quickly and leaves the room, hoping the former occupants are somewhere in Scotland at the moment, delivering a message to a certain general in Duncan's army. He hops back down the stairs and points his nose again in the direction of the fresh air.

Turn to section 32.

Section 76

* **76** *

Shea enters the passageway that smells of sulphur. The experience is all too familiar, and his mind drifts back to Muspellheim, where he spent time in another dungeon cell. The tunnel curves slowly left as he walks, his mind in another world altogether. Before he knows it, Shea is standing in a large chamber lit by pools of boiling brimstone and gas jets.

"No!" he says out loud. "What am I doing here?" Shea turns to run and is startled to find himself face to face with a short, fat, yellow human-shaped creature with a wide smiling mouth and way too many eyes.

"Thou art my guest," the creature lisps, in answer to Shea's unspoken question. Behind it stands a group of things about half his size but twice as ugly. "I am Pholantus," it continues, "Keeper of the Firemount furnace, so to speak, otherwise called a demon of the pits. Smoke is a love I raise with fuming sighs." It blows a smoke ring in the air and extends a six-fingered hand toward Harold. "And thou art Harold Shea. I am as honored to make thy acquaintance as thou art mine."

Reluctantly, Harold shakes Pholantus'

Section 76

hand, saying, "Hey, how do you know who I am?"

The demon gestures toward the bubbling pool of lava. "I see much. A friend of thine hight Dolan came once unto me. I fear he spoke of thee naught but ill. Great then was my surprise to find thee here on Setebos' isle. But lo, let's have a bit of witty verse . . . Eskimo Nell, perhaps?"

That last statement is disturbing. Shea once recited that poem in Faerie. This guy seems to know everything about him. "I'm not really in the mood for poetry," complains Shea.

Roll 3 D6 and compare the result with Harold's Charisma value.

If the total of the dice is the same as or lower than Harold's Charisma, turn to section 91.

If the total of the dice is higher, turn to section 34.

Section 77

* **77** *

Shea pulls Belphebe near him. Three bedraggled sailors come running toward them. A sudden bolt of lightning from the witch roasts the sailors right in front of Shea. Goblin spears fall onto the sand nearby.

"Hold my hand, Belphebe . . . you, too, Votsy," Shea says desperately. "I'm gonna try the spell Chalmers gave me to use on Dolan. . . . Brace yourselves." He begins to gesture wildly with his free hand as he mumbles the dangerous words of the incantation. It has worked before, destroying one of the most powerful magicians in the land of Faerie. It might work now and destroy the witch . . . and possibly everyone else as well.

Roll 3 D6 and compare the result to Harold's Wisdom value.

If the total of the dice is the same as or lower than Harold's Wisdom, turn to section 55.

If the total is higher, turn to section 39.

* 78 *

Shea wonders if he is a victim of doublethink as he decides to investigate the death smell . . . because the tunnel that smells pleasant probably means danger. Then again, maybe it doesn't. He steps timidly into the smelly passage, holding the torch before him. The tunnel winds first left, then right. After about fifty feet, it opens up into a small room. The stench of death is even stronger.

It is easy to see why. The room is full of decaying goblin bodies organized into rows. Some of the bodies are fresh, others mere skeletons covered with rusting armor or holding weapons across their chests. A rat scurries away from the light of his torch. As Shea jumps in alarm, a glint of light at the rear of the room catches his eye.

Gingerly, Shea picks his way between the bodies and finds a wooden door with a brass plate centered on its rough surface. Engraved on the plate are some symbols he can't read. He tries the door but it won't budge. It is locked.

In the dirt, Shea spots a small bent spike that seems to be the right size to pick the lock.

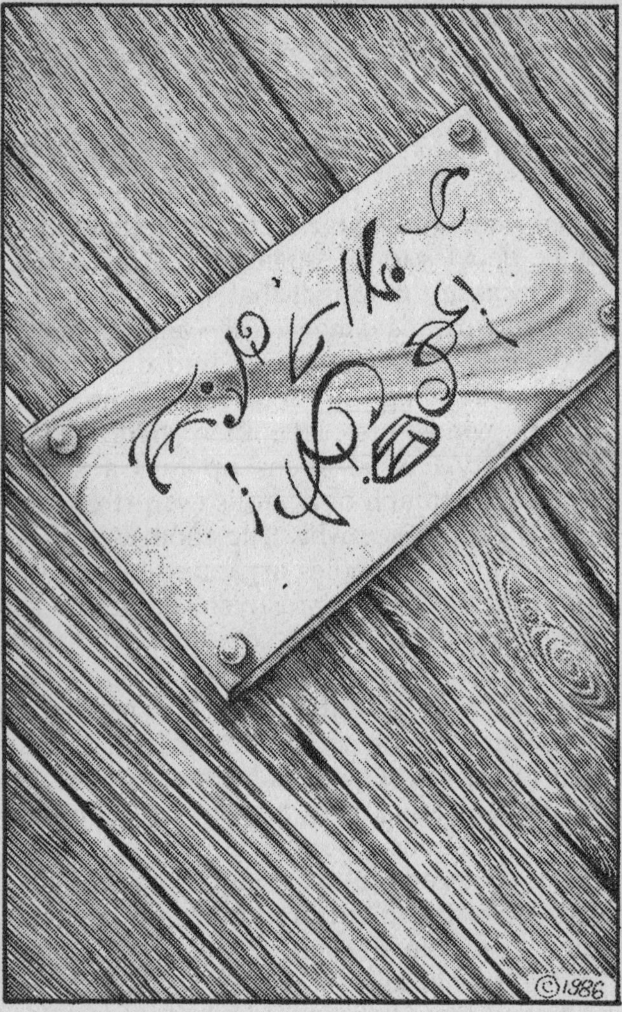
©1986

Section 78

If Harold tries to pick the lock and enters the next room, turn to section 86.

If Harold returns to the main passageway, return to section 60 and choose a different corridor.

* 79 *

Shea struggles to his feet and dusts himself off. He rubs a sore elbow. This business is dangerous! The goblins at the top of the hill begin yelling assorted oaths. A large rock crashes nearby. Two more missiles hurled by the angry goblins convince him that this isn't a place to hang around. Shea runs off down a shoulder of the mountain and in among some brambles and dead trees. He struggles down a ridge, up a cinder pile, and then back down again to make his way along a dry gully. Soon the voices begin to fade behind him.

He pauses a moment to catch his breath, then resumes his flight, running at first, for what seems like an hour. Shea crashes now and again into a clump of prickly thornbushes. Then his legs begin to ache, and he slows to a steady walk. There has been no sign of the enemy since he left the path.

Turn to section 14.

* 80 *

"Pentacles far and pentacles near,
 I forthwith command you, disappear!
 Shemhamporesh!"

The door creaks inward slightly. Harold gives it a gentle push and it swings open.

Turn to section 63.

* 81 *

Shea grabs the club from the table and stands ready to meet the attack of the onrushing goblin. It swings its club high, aiming for Harold's head. He ducks, and in the same motion brings his own club up with a thud into the goblin's chest. It stumbles backward. His next opponent has run around the far side of the tomb, and Shea meets its club in mid-swing with his own. The clubs come together with a crack that numbs his fingers.

By now a third goblin has entered the room, screaming oaths at the top of its voice. Shea dances around behind the table and pushes it over. The goblin runs into it and flips over to the floor. Shea delivers a crushing blow to its head and it falls dead. The next goblin clips Shea on the side of the head, and he spins around dizzily.

Miraculously keeping his balance, Harold barely has time to parry a blow from a goblin with the end of his club. The creature leaves itself open, and Shea kicks it fiercely in the shins. Down it goes. A fifth goblin storms in, and somehow Shea maneuvers himself between it and another foe, then ducks at the

Section 81

right moment. They knock each other to the ground.

Shea leans back against the table, panting, not believing his luck. He hears the clatter of more goblins coming his way and wisely walks over to the escape hole at the rear of the room.

Turn to section 74.

* 82 *

Belphebe, Bitter-Root, and the fire disappear behind Harold. The hippo seems to be picking up speed. Between its bouncing gait and slippery skin, it is all he can do to stay on top. Shea yells out commands: "Stop! Turn right! Turn left!" He kicks it with his heels, but all to no avail. The hippo continues its mad flight, splashing and bouncing down the stream.

A branch slaps Harold in the face, nearly unseating him. Moments later, the hippo swerves to the left. Before he can compensate, Shea feels himself slipping helplessly and falling down the far side of the beast. He lands with a breathtaking thud on the gravel bank.

Subtract one hit point from Harold's total on the record sheet.

The hippo crashes off into the darkness. Shea groans and struggles to his feet. Nothing seems to be broken. He stumbles back along the stream toward the smoldering fire.

"I've changed my mind," he says with as

Section 82

much dignity as he can muster. "I think I'll just hold onto that unicorn's tail after all."

Turn to section 28.

* 83 *

Shea takes off his coat and slips the mail vest over his head. At first it feels a bit snug around the shoulders, but it immediately softens and conforms magically to the shape of his body. It seems to have almost no weight. The vest instills a sense of confidence in Shea, and as he puts on his coat over it, he is certain that he has found a magic vest.

Add a −1 magic vest to Harold's list of possessions. While he is wearing the vest, subtract one point from any damage Harold receives.

Return to section 86.

* 84 *

To his amazement, Harold's hand passes right through the staff and robe. His fingertips brush against an unseen glass object, knocking it to the floor with a crash. Blue smoke rises from the hissing mess and awakens Caliban. The baby lets out a dreadful howl.

"Damn!" curses Shea as he steps back from the smoking mess. "It was an illusion."

"Methinks we'd best leave," says Belphebe urgently as she tugs at his sleeve. Across the room, two goblins wearing what look like burlap sacks appear from behind a dark curtain. They see the intruders and scream in high-pitched voices as they run to the baby's crib.

Goblin nursemaids, muses Shea as he and Belphebe hot-foot it around the far side of the room and sprint for the door. Before they can reach it, however, some unexpected watchdogs race in from outside and square off in front of them. Shea finds himself face to face with two snarling wolves. It is obvious there can be no escape without a fight.

Section 84

TWO WOLVES

To hit Shea: 13   To be hit: 12   Hit points: 6 each

Damage per bite: D6+1. Shea does D6 damage with a club. If he has a sword, he can do D6+1 damage.

As long as there are two wolves, Belphebe keeps one wolf busy so that only one wolf attacks Harold each round.

After each round, Harold may attempt to escape. Roll 3 D6 and compare the result to Harold's Dexterity value.

If the total of the dice is the same as or lower than Harold's Dexterity, turn to section 46.

If the total is higher, the fight continues.

If Harold wins using a +1 sword, turn to section 56.

If Harold wins using a club, turn to section 44.

If Harold is killed, turn to section 29.

* 85 *

Shea lands with a crash in the thorny scrub. It is thicker than it looks from above, and his left foot catches in a branch while the rest of his body plows on through the thorns. At last he comes to rest, hanging upside down by his foot. Shea's cheeks and hands sting with numerous tiny scratches. He can just reach the ground with his hands. Pushing himself up on his hands, he tries to free his foot.

Shea begins bouncing up and down like a ball on a string. His foot comes loose and he crashes heavily to the ground. He rubs his ankle and struggles to his feet, only to find himself surrounded by goblins. Two particularly ugly dark green goblins grab him roughly by the arms. With a spear at his back, Shea is led back to the campsite and retied to the pole.

Shea contemplates his misfortune, taking small satisfaction from the fact that his captors seem to have quite a bonfire going. The unfortunate goblin whom Shea had tricked is also tied to a pole.

Hungry, wet, and in pain, Shea sleeps fitfully that night.

Turn to section 47.

Section 86

* 86 *

Shea picks up the spike and begins fiddling with the lock. To his surprise, he immediately hears a faint click and the door creaks open. He picks up his torch and cautiously walks through the door. The flickering yellow light reveals a large sarcophagus in the center of the room. The walls form a rough circle and are carved out of smooth black rock, almost glassy in appearance. There is a thick layer of dust all over the floor. On a table near the tomb, he sees a small helmet, a mail vest, and a polished war club with a rusted steel handle.

Shea inspects the rest of the room but finds only a small hole leading out the back. Something about the vest makes him pick it up. There is a clank behind him in the room of the dead. He stares at the door but hears no more. Shea's attention returns to the vest. It looks too small, but as he holds it against his body, it seems to grow to his dimensions.

If Harold wishes to try on the mail vest, turn to section 83.

Suddenly, there is a clamor in the next

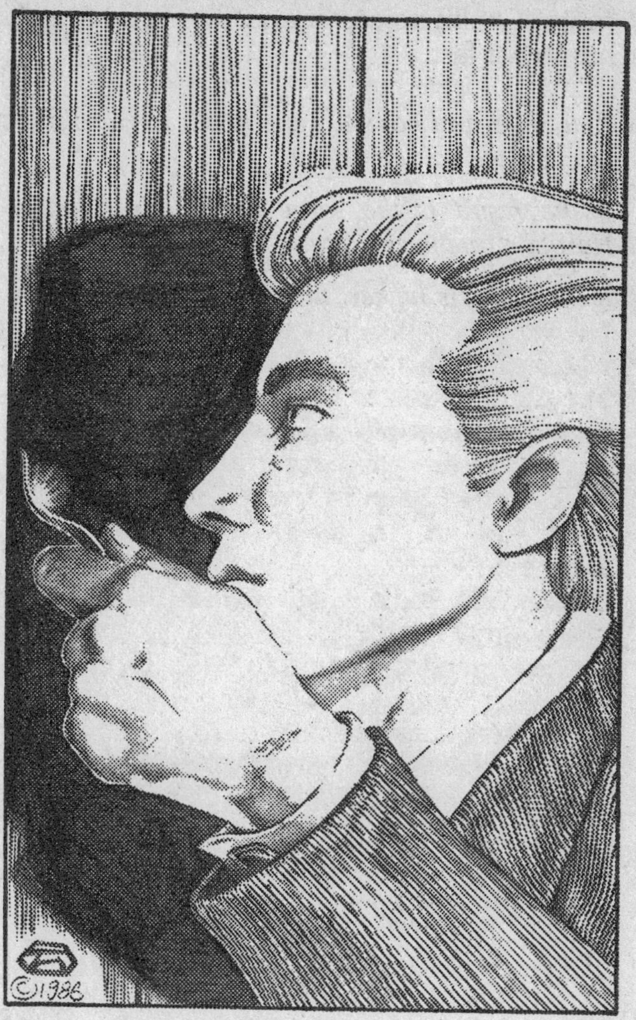
©1986

Section 86

room. Goblin voices cry out in anger. Shea has to act fast.

Roll 3 D6 and compare the result to Harold's Intelligence value.

If the result is the same as or lower than Harold's Intelligence, turn to section 74.

If the result is higher, turn to section 68.

* 87 *

Beads of sweat pop out on Shea's forehead before the fight even begins. His épée is one thing; this heavy iron trident is another. Pholantus circles around him threateningly. This is as much like fencing as football is like baseball . . . both sports require players and balls.

The demon lunges at him. Shea parries with a resounding clang and tries a riposte, but his weapon is so heavy that the demon easily deflects the effort. Pholantus advances and Shea gives ground. The sparring continues without result until Shea slips on a rock. As he struggles to regain his balance, the demon lunges and the tip of his trident pokes painfully into Shea's left arm.

Pholantus clucks with glee and smacks the flat of his trident against Shea's head. There is a blinding flash of light, and Harold drops his weapon and falls to the floor. As he rolls to recover, the points of the demon's trident tear into his stomach. The pain is excruciating.

"Farewell, sweet playfellow, pray now for

Section 87

thy soul!" gloats Pholantus. The dull red light of the room begins to fade.

Turn to section 29.

* 88 *

Malovio leads the way through the prickly undergrowth with such speed that Shea is amazed. The little goblin trudges on tirelessly, as though they are being chased by an army. But then, maybe they *are* being chased by an army. They stop to drink from a stream.

"Hey, Mal," Shea says, "when are you going to find us that meal?" His empty stomach is tying itself in knots.

"Soon, Harold, I know a secret place." On they go through endless fields of scrub till they come to a grove of dead trees. There is an eerie look about it. The leafless trees stand like obelisks in a graveyard. Malovio plops down on a fallen log.

"You, sir, make fire. I shall bring game," says the goblin. "Know ye that I'm a great hunter."

"So what's to hunt?" asks Shea. "I haven't seen a single animal all day."

Malovio bends down and picks up a pointed stick. "One must know the land to find the game!" he answers casually, and then begins walking off. "Make it a big fire!"

Section 88

says the goblin as it disappears behind a bush.

Shea gathers wood for a fire, but with his lighter gone he is afraid he will end up rubbing two sticks together to get it started. He stumbles across an old fire pit and carefully lays the wood in the middle. He is pleased to discover several pieces of flint which somebody, or something, has left behind.

It takes him a good bit of smashing stones together to find the right combination, and even longer to persuade a little mound of dry moss to start smoking. Soon, however, he has a fine crackling fire going.

Malovio comes walking proudly back into camp. Harold shudders when he sees what the goblin has hanging from the stick over his shoulder. A brace of fat rats! Neither of them has a knife, so the catch is roasted the way it came, fur and all. Shea doesn't really care. He is too hungry to object.

While supper sizzles, Malovio digs under a pile of branches and produces a small, well-used copper kettle.

"Stew?" asks the goblin.

"Y'know," says Shea, "I'd rather have beer! You fill that thing with water, and I'll put my magical powers to work on it."

Malovio's eyes light up. "Most assuredly!"

Shea gathers some grasses that resemble

Section 88

barley and scratches out the formula for alcohol on the end of a stick. He can make finer stuff with sugar cubes, but one has to make do. Shea sighs.

Malovio returns with the kettle of water. Shea dumps in the grasses and begins to stir, chanting:

> "Beer, beer, beautiful beer,
>   Fill this pot up with it,
>   Clear up to here!"

A corny verse Polacek once nearly got in trouble using, but it ought to work in these circumstances. A brown froth begins forming in the pot. Shea sticks his finger in the mix. Not bad, he thinks to himself. He and the goblin take turns taking large drafts from the kettle.

"Fair magic," says Malovio, smiling, "thy liquor is unearthly."

Shea thinks it has a muddy aftertaste and is very "earthly," but it packs a punch. Soon he and the goblin are old friends, laughing and telling each other inane jokes. The roasted rats taste as good as gourmet chicken. When the meal is done, the goblin goes for more water and Shea brews up a second batch of beer. As night settles in around them, the goblin grows maudlin.

"Before that witch Sycorax, our life on

Section 88

this isle was full-easy. In Firemount we lived, and served the great drake, who was little enough trouble. Yet now we are but stevedores and whipping-boys."

So the goblins aren't too fond of the witch either, muses Shea.

"Now lead I the renegade life, and 'tisn't an easy trip," complains Malovio.

"Who is this great drake?" asks Shea, seeing a potential ally.

"At the root of the Firemount now sleeps a mighty fire drake, a hot and fiery thing. Yet Sycorax accurst it, and full seven years hath it slept." Malovio sighs heavily. "And now slaves we are. The life of a goblin is not easy."

Malovio takes a long drink from the kettle, grins, and passes out. The fire dies, and soon Shea too falls asleep.

It is past noon the next day when Harold regains consciousness. His head throbs. Too much beer, no doubt. Malovio is nowhere to be found, and Shea decides to set out in search of Belphebe. He leaves the grove and heads for the nearest hill. Some movement catches his attention and he quickly hides behind a tree trunk. It is fortunate he did not sleep longer. A party of twenty or more goblins comes stomping up and mills around the fire. Shea carefully edges away from the campsite, leaving the goblins behind.

Section 88

He climbs the hill but sees nothing more than bramble bushes and dead trees.

Turn to section 14.

Section 89

* 89 *

Harold takes the stone, which proves to be very warm.

"Now what am I supposed to do with this?" asks Shea.

"Keep it well, for I seest through the dark abysm of time!" answers the demon. "When thou speakest unto the fire drake, thy answer shall reveal itself."

At the moment, Shea has no intention of speaking with a fire drake, but he smiles and pops the stone into his pocket.

"Thanks, old boy!" he replies.

Add the stone to Harold's list of possessions. If ever Shea attempts to cast a spell to control the fire drake, subtract 5 to his total dice roll for that spell.

"Thou hast kept me long enough from my business, so now farewell." Pholantus bows. "Ephesia will show you out."

One of the ugly creatures leads Shea around the room and points to a small tunnel.

Turn to section 74.

* 90 *

Feeling his head to see if any hair remains, Shea turns and runs out of the room as fast as his feet can carry him. Blind terror carries him up the dark passageway. He can't see and loses his footing; he trips over an unseen rock but never stops moving. Right behind him, the thundering beat of the drake's wings follows his trail.

Shea runs wildly into the large entry chamber and hops on his broom. He rattles off his chant at 78 rpm and has barely finished when the fire drake crashes in behind him. The broom rises off the floor and shoots out the mouth of the cave with Shea leaning over like a high-speed motorcyclist. Moments later the drake roars after him, beating its enormous wings to gain altitude.

Shea tries a few aerobatic tricks to get the dragon off his tail. He pulls up into a stall and then spins straight toward the earth, pulling out at the last moment. He levels off just above the treetops and dodges up and down the valleys, but the beast, although not as maneuverable as Shea, is a match for him in speed.

Maybe, thinks Shea, just getting this mon-

Section 90

ster to the scene of the battle will help, and he begins leading it across the island to where the battle with Sycorax is raging.

Belphebe curses as a rock smashes into her shin. Ever since Harold mysteriously departed, she, Polacek, and Snag have been in control of the army of spirits, sailors, and fairies, and it hasn't worked any too well. Polacek keeps leafing through the magic book and attempts to cast spells which invariably fail or, worse, backfire and kill several of their own number.

Snag proves to be a natural leader, dividing his forces into platoons of fighting sailors who go into battle with knives, swords, spears, rocks, and belaying pins. Each time the forces of the witch make a move to outflank, Snag responds by sending in a counterattack that drives her minions back.

Sycorax is persistent, and she drives her army of goblins forward. Although Belphebe and her archers, and Snag and his sword- and spearmen, take a fearful toll of the enemy, the witch seems to have an endless supply of dark green, willing-to-die creatures. Snag is forced to give ground.

The spirit cave is overwhelmed, and they retreat over the ridge to the next hill . . . and then to the next, and the next. A bolt from the witch drives Quamoclit into the heart of

Section 90

a pine tree. Belphebe winces as she hears the spirit scream. The sailors retreat at a command from Snag, and all, including Belphebe, run at full speed over the last hill that separates them from the sea. The huntress searches the sky in vain for a sign of her husband.

A brief respite is achieved when Polacek casts a spell that actually works. For several minutes, a large cloud of noxious yellow smoke pours out of a tree stump. As it drifts over the goblins, they reel back in agony.

"Phosgene," says Polacek, smiling. "It's an old trick the Huns had in the First World War."

Belphebe looks at him with a puzzled expression. Harold told her of a world war, but she never heard of this. She is more concerned about the fact that there are only seven arrows left in her quiver, and the sailors who stand by her side all seem to have equally low supplies of missiles.

There is a sudden shout, and all faces look skyward. Coming over the crest of the hill is a monster of enormous proportions. Another of the witch's servants, no doubt. They are surely doomed. Belphebe puts her hand to her forehead and groans.

Polacek beings dancing up and down and shakes her. "It's Harold," he exclaims, pointing at the tiny figure on the broom just ahead

Section 90

of the flying creature. Belphebe looks up in awe.

Shea is horrified to see the vast number of goblins still swarming over the forests below. His heart sinks when he sees the spirit cave overrun. Is he too late? He banks to the left and swoops up over the last row of hills, with the fire drake following close behind.

There they are! The good guys sure have their backs to the wall. Now, how is he going to get this angry fire drake to help his cause? He pulls the broom into a sharp wingover and zooms in low over the army of goblins. Many of them look up and shake their fists at him while others chuck rocks and spears into the air. The fire drake stays on his tail and, just as Shea makes a sharp turn toward the sea, a goblin spear catches the monster in the eye. It lets out a horrendous roar and belches out a blast of orange flame that engulfs hundreds of unfortunate goblins.

Shea grins, puts the broom into a tight turn, and circles low over the army of sailors. He hears a cheer rise up from below. Another strike like that and the witch will be out of business (and goblins). He spots Belphebe and waves triumphantly.

The drake is again on his tail. Shea flies out over the sea, maneuvering the monster back in for a second attack. This time, Shea catches sight of the red robe of the witch and

Section 90

aims straight at her. Suddenly a bolt of electric blue light shoots up from where the witch stands and sizzles past Shea. It envelops the fire drake and there is the crackle of shooting sparks. The drake shudders. Its wings stop beating and it veers off to the left. Shea finds himself directly in the path of the monster as it falls to the ground like a shot-down bomber.

The drake's tail slaps him hard and knocks him off the broom. The beast plows into a mass of trees with a dreadful crash, snapping them off like matchsticks. Shea is thrown, miraculously, onto the top of a sand dune.

He lays there, stunned, struggling to catch his breath. He is still alive, he thinks to himself. It could be worse. He rolls dizzily down to the base of the dune and sits up, trying to orient himself. At last he sees Belphebe, jumping up and down and motioning to him. Shea struggles to his feet and runs through a rain of goblin-thrown rocks to reach her side.

Turn to section 13.

* 91 *

Pholantus sniffs the air haughtily with his warty nose. "So be it. Thou hast kept me long enough from my business, and now farewell." Pholantus bows. "Ephesia will show you out."

One of the ugly creatures leads Shea around the room and points to a small tunnel. A very curious encounter, thinks Shea.

Turn to section 74.

Section 92

* 92 *

Shea grabs the club from the table and stands ready to meet the attack of the onrushing goblin. It swings its club high, aiming for Harold's head. Shea ducks, and in the same motion brings his own club up with a thud into the goblin's chest. It stumbles backward. Shea manages to circle around the sarcophagus. He pushes the table over, sending the helmet clattering to the floor. The next goblin smashes into it and flips over onto its back. Shea calmly turns and walks over to the small exit hole he saw earlier.

Turn to section 74.

Section 93

* 93 *

More cautiously than ever, Shea follows Belphebe's carefully chosen footsteps. She adroitly sidesteps a pile of human skulls. After a few fearful moments, they navigate the room and are once again in a narrow tunnel. It winds down and to the left, then empties out into a much larger cavern.

"Methinks down is the way to travel," whispers Belphebe. Shea agrees.

Turn to section 54.

* 94 *

Beads of sweat pop out on Shea's forehead before the fight even begins. His épée is one thing; this heavy iron trident is another. Pholantus circles around him threateningly. This is as much like fencing as football is like baseball . . . both sports require players and balls.

The demon lunges at him. Shea parries with a resounding clang and tries a riposte, but his weapon is so heavy that the demon easily deflects the effort. Pholantus advances and Shea gives ground. The sparring continues without result until Shea slips on a rock. As he struggles to regain his balance, the demon lunges and the points of his trident poke painfully into Shea's left arm.

Pholantus clucks with glee. Shea manages to beat off the next attack and clubs the demon in the face with the wrong end of his weapon.

"Foul!" screams Pholantus, staggering backward. Shea glances to his left and sees the entrance to a small tunnel.

"So long, old boy. Sorry I can't stay for the finish."

Turn to section 74.

CROSSROADS™ ADVENTURES

- [ ] 56400-6 DAVID DRAKE'S THE DRAGON LORD — $3.50
  56401-4 STORM OF DUST by Neil Randall — Canada $4.50
- [ ] 56402-2 ROBERT SILVERBERG'S MAJIPOOR — $3.50
  56403-0 REVOLT ON MAJIPOOR
  by Matt Costello — Canada $4.50
- [ ] 56404-9 ANNE MCCAFFREY'S PERN — $3.50
  56405-7 DRAGONHARPER
  by Jody Lynn Nye — Canada $4.50

Coming in September

- [ ] 56406-5 C.J. CHERRYH'S MORGAINE — $3.50
  56407-3 THE WITCHFIRES OF LETH
  by Dan Greenberg — Canada $4.50

Coming in October

- [ ] 56408-1 L. SPRAGUE DE CAMP AND
  FLETCHER PRATT'S
  THE INCOMPLETE ENCHANTER — $3.50
  56409-X PROSPERO'S ISLE by Tom Wham — Canada $4.50

Coming in November

- [ ] 56410-3 STEVEN BRUST'S JHEREG — $3.50
  56411-1 DZURLORD
  by Adventure Architects — Canada $4.50

Buy them at your local bookstore or use this handy coupon:
Clip and mail this page with your order

ST. MARTIN'S/TOR BOOKS—Reader Service Dept.
175 Fifth Avenue, New York, NY 10010

Please send me the book(s) I have checked above. I am enclosing
$_____ (please add $1.00 to cover postage and handling). Send
check or money order only—no cash or C.O.D.'s.

Mr./Mrs./Miss _____

Address _____

City _____ State/Zip _____

Please allow six weeks for delivery. Prices subject to change without notice.

FRED SABERHAGEN

- [ ] 55327-6 BERSERKER BASE — $3.95
  55328-4 — Canada $4.95
- [ ] 55322-5 BERSERKER: BLUE DEATH (Trade) — $6.95
  55323-3 — Canada $8.95
- [ ] 55318-7 THE BERSERKER THRONE — $3.50
  55319-5 — Canada $4.50
- [ ] 55312-8 THE BERSERKER WARS — $3.50
  55313-6 — Canada $4.50
- [ ] 48564-6 EARTH DESCENDED — $2.95
- [ ] 55335-7 THE FIRST BOOK OF SWORDS — $3.50
  55336-5 — Canada $4.50
- [ ] 55331-4 THE SECOND BOOK OF SWORDS — $3.50
  55332-2 — Canada $4.50
- [ ] 55333-0 THE THIRD BOOK OF SWORDS — $3.50
  55334-9 — Canada $4.50
- [ ] 55309-8 THE MASK OF THE SUN — $2.95
  55310-1 — Canada $3.95
- [ ] 52550-7 AN OLD FRIEND OF THE FAMILY — $3.50
  52551-5 — Canada $4.50
- [ ] 55290-3 THE WATER OF THOUGHT — $2.95
  55291-1 — Canada $3.50

Buy them at your local bookstore or use this handy coupon:
Clip and mail this page with your order

ST. MARTIN'S/TOR BOOKS—Reader Service Dept.
175 Fifth Avenue, New York, NY 10010

Please send me the book(s) I have checked above. I am enclosing
$_____ (please add $1.00 to cover postage and handling).
Send check or money order only—no cash or C.O.D.'s.

Mr./Mrs./Miss _____

Address _____

City _____ State/Zip _____

Please allow six weeks for delivery. Prices subject to change without notice.